THE HARBOR HOUSE
A THISTLE ISLAND NOVEL

MIA KENT

The Harbor House

By Mia Kent

© Copyright 2022

ALL RIGHTS RESERVED

No part of this book may be used or reproduced in any manner whatsoever without written permission except in the case of brief quotations embodied in critical articles and reviews.

This is a work of fiction. Names, characters, places, and incidents are products of the author's imagination or are used fictitiously. Any resemblance to actual events, locales, organizations, or persons, living or dead, is entirely coincidental.

Cover design by Craig Thomas (coversbycraigthomas@gmail.com)

GET YOUR FREE BOOK!

To instantly receive a free copy of *The Inn at Dolphin Bay*, the first novel in my most popular series, join my Reader Club at www.miakent.com/dolphin.

CHAPTER 1

"Happy birthday dear Robyn, happy birthday to you! And many more, till you're five hundred and seventy-fouuuuur." Layla drew out the last word with a wicked grin as she set a vanilla-frosted cupcake on Robyn Wright's desk beside her proof copy of the latest issue of *Coastal Weddings*.

"Thanks," Robyn said, blowing out an imaginary candle on top of the cupcake before peeling off the wrapper and taking a bite, elbowing her keyboard out of the way as she did so. Work could wait. Sugar could not.

"So tell me," Layla said, raising one eyebrow as she leaned against Robyn's desk and folded her arms across her chest. "How old are you this year? Thirty-nine again?"

"To tell you the truth, I'm a little bit tired of being thirty-nine," Robyn said between bites of cupcake. She gave her coworker a thoughtful look. "I thought this year I'd live dangerously. Take myself back to the glory days of thirty-seven."

Layla snorted as she picked up the proof copy of the magazine and began flicking through it idly. "Keep it up and pretty soon you'll be younger than me." Then she set the magazine down again with a sigh. "Besides, I want to be you when I grow up. You're the best writer this place has ever seen, and don't even get me started on that man of yours." She shook her head. "Help a girl out—where can I find one of them for myself?"

Robyn let out a light laugh, ignoring the pang of anxiety in the pit of her stomach at the mention of Keith, her significant other of a decade. With his broad shoulders, devil-may-care smile, and honey-brown eyes that sparkled every time they caught the light, most women found him appealing, and after all this time, Robyn was used to the jealous looks being thrown her way whenever they were out on the town. He even had a personality to match his looks—charming but kind, successful but generous.

From the outside, it looked like Robyn had found the perfect man.

"So did you hear the news?" Layla asked as Robyn finished the last bite of her cupcake and tossed the wrapper into the trash can beneath her desk. When she shook her head, her coworker poked her head out of the cubicle, looked both ways, and then lowered her voice as she added, "Word on the street is that we're heading for more cutbacks." The lightness in her tone did little to hide the flash of fear in her eyes. "How many people have we lost so far this year?"

"Thirteen." Robyn leaned back in her chair and rubbed her temples. "All good people."

"Yeah, well, not according to Melody." Layla's tone had turned bitter, her eyes sparking with anger. "And the rest of us have had to work overtime to pick up the slack. How is that fair?"

"You and I both know it's not so simple," Robyn said, even though she privately agreed with her friend's assessment. They were both writers for Coastal Publications, a print and digital media company that published a number of magazines, including the popular *Coastal Weddings* and *Coastal Designs*. The company had been around for decades, but the advent of the internet and the resulting hit to distribution numbers for printed newspapers and magazines around the world had caused a monetary crisis that was starting to come to a head.

In other words, the company was running out of money. And the employees—including several of Robyn's friends, talented writers in their own right—were always the first casualties.

Robyn had worked for Coastal Publications for the entirety of her career, starting as an intern after graduating college with a degree in journalism and working her way up to senior writer. Over the past twenty years, she'd had a front-row seat to the ever-declining number of people who subscribed to their magazines, and even though she hadn't always agreed with editor-in-chief Melody Carson's decisions on who had to be let go, Robyn knew the woman was doing what she believed to be best for the company's survival.

Layla knew this too. But that didn't make the reality of the situation—or the precariousness of their positions at the company—any easier a pill to swallow.

"You know what? Let's focus on the positive right now." Layla swatted her hand in the air, erasing the topic of conversation. Her eyes took on a mischievous gleam again as she refocused her attention on

Robyn. "On to more pressing issues." She paused dramatically, and Robyn, immediately sensing where this was going, felt her stomach sink a few more inches toward her feet. "Is tonight the night?"

"I hope so." The words tasted like ash on Robyn's tongue, though she did her best to keep the smile on her face. "He's been hinting around at it for months, and what better day than today?" The smile grew wider, and for a moment—for a blessed, blissful moment—Robyn almost believed what she was saying, could almost *feel* the excitement welling up inside her. "We've got reservations at Salvatore's."

Layla gasped, then clapped her hands together in delight. "The fanciest restaurant in town? Girl, you *know* it's happening. I can't wait to hear all the details—and see that gorgeous ring for myself." She stretched out her hand, gazing longingly at her own bare ring finger. "And who knows?" she added with a wink. "By the time I'm thirty-seven, maybe it'll be my turn."

Then she turned and headed for her neighboring cubicle, calling back over her shoulder, "Gotta run. My article on beach-themed weddings on a budget isn't going to write itself, you know, and I don't want to make myself Melody's next target by missing my deadline."

Then she was gone, leaving Robyn to stare blankly at her computer screen as she imagined what was in store for her this evening—and how much of her conversation with Layla had been true, and how much had been wishful thinking. The scales definitely tipped in the latter direction, she thought with a sigh as she flicked open the proof copy of *Coastal Weddings* once more and retrieved her red pen from beside her keyboard.

Ever since Melody had made significant cutbacks to the company's editing department, Robyn had been tasked with picking up some of the extra work of combing through each magazine prior to publication for typos or layout errors—for longer hours and a zero-dollar pay raise. But truth be told, she didn't mind all that much. She was committed to the company and wanted to do everything in her power to help keep the magazines churning off the press. Writing was her passion, her lifeblood. She couldn't imagine doing anything else, but jobs in the field were increasingly hard to come by. If Coastal Publications closed its doors, Robyn would be left out in the cold.

Quite possibly permanently.

With that in mind, she spent the better part of the next hour hunched over her desk, scrutinizing each page, every so often using her pen to make a correction or highlight an issue that needed to be fixed. So engrossed was she in her work that she didn't hear the sound of footsteps approaching her cubicle until Melody's familiar perfume filled the space.

"Robyn, do you have a moment?"

She looked up to find her boss standing behind her, arms crossed, normally friendly face pinched with worry. Robyn had seen that same expression several times over the past few months and knew immediately that the rumor mill had once again been correct.

Cutbacks.

Who would be the next victims?

Robyn hated giving her opinion, wished Melody didn't ask such a monumental task of her. Nobody in the office knew that she had a heads-up on the hiring and firing process… though these days, there wasn't much of the former going on. But as the company's head writer and longest-serving employee, Robyn's insights were invaluable. According to Melody, at least. Robyn was certain Layla and the rest of her coworkers wouldn't quite see it that way.

Layla tried to catch Robyn's eye as she followed

Melody out of the long row of cubicles toward her office, and she could see the rest of the staff exchanging wary looks as the editor-in-chief passed by, expression grave. Some turned sympathetic eyes on Robyn, believing she was on a death march to Melody's office, already planning out what words of comfort they would offer her when she emerged five minutes from now, teary-eyed, like so many others had in recent weeks.

But Robyn's job was safe… for now, at least. Melody had assured her of that long ago, told her she was too valuable an employee to lose.

It had been a boost to Robyn's ego. Something that was hard to come by these days, especially given what the next few hours would bring.

"Come on in," Melody said, standing back to usher Robyn into her office. The space was much like the woman who occupied it, Robyn thought as she took a seat across from the editor-in-chief's pristine desk. With its floor-to-ceiling windows overlooking a row of stunning flowering trees, cream-and-white décor, and minimalist design, the office was as chic and no-nonsense as Melody was, with her sleek chin-length bob, subtle but professional-looking makeup, and polished outfits.

Robyn, whose wavy brown hair tended to have a

slightly flyaway look—a much kinder word than "frizzy," she'd decided long ago—always felt frumpy in her presence, and she realized now that she was smoothing her hands over and over a wrinkle in her pants as she waited for her boss to take the seat across from her. Forcing herself to stop, she clenched her hands in her lap instead, holding her breath as she waited for Melody to begin speaking and hoping against hope that Layla wasn't going to be on the chopping block this time.

"So, here we are again." Melody's tone was laced with sadness as she crossed one leg over the other and fixed her gaze on Robyn, who shifted uncomfortably in her chair. As she did so, she caught a glimpse of her coworkers huddled in clumps around their cubicles, their expressions strained as they watched the scene unfolding inside while pretending to be going about their business as usual.

"The quarterly reports are in," Melody continued, "and the numbers are... well, I guess the only word I can come up with is abysmal." She tucked a strand of hair behind one ear and shook her head. "And that's despite the ramp-up in marketing, the special offers we've given our loyal readers, the decision to cut our number of issues almost in half..." Her voice trailed off as she stared down at the financial report on her desk, tracing one perfectly manicured fingernail down the rows of numbers that Robyn was now straining to see.

Melody exhaled heavily and pressed her fingers to her lips for a moment as her eyes wandered to the rows of cubicles. "The board is requiring more layoffs—and this time, they've asked me to be extreme."

Robyn winced. *Here we go again*, she thought.

"And I've gone over the numbers again and again, and I can't see any other way." Melody set down the paper she was perusing and folded her hands on the desk. "To keep the magazine running, we need our writers, of course. But we also need to cut costs, so that means we'll be keeping our most junior writers for now, and letting go of our senior staff. Temporarily, I hope. Despite what the reports say, I remain optimistic about our future."

Robyn stared at her boss, certain she had misheard. "And by senior staff, you mean…"

"You." The word was blunt almost to the point of being painful. "And five others." Then Melody's expression softened. "I'm so sorry, Robyn. Believe me when I say I wish it didn't have to be this way. But." She held up a finger. "I also don't make promises that I can't keep. And while my hand is being forced right now, I've moved some things around and come up with room in the budget for a part-time freelance writer. Ten hours a week, maybe more if our circulation numbers increase." She gave Robyn a genuine smile. "So what do you say? Will you take the job?"

Take the job? Robyn could scarcely believe the words coming out of the other woman's mouth, as if losing her job—her well-paying job with benefits and retirement—and then snatching up whatever scraps the company decided to throw at her in the form of part-time grunt work was a *privilege*.

Twenty-two years at this company. Twenty-two *years* of hard work and dedication and genuine passion for the things she accomplished each day.

All down the toilet in a matter of seconds.

She opened her mouth to say no, *never*, the sentence hot on her lips. And then she immediately closed it again.

Gas for her car. Food on the table. Credit card payments.

Robyn's personal crisis wouldn't cause the bills to stop piling up in the mailbox. Sure, she could rely on Keith for help… but only for so long. It wasn't like they were married. Or even engaged.

Another pang at that last thought.

"Fine. I'll take it." Robyn's hands were clenched into fists.

Melody seemed not to notice. In fact, she looked relieved. As if she had done her part in keeping her word that Robyn's job was safe.

"Good, good. *Wonderful*," she said happily. "I'll draw up the contract for you this afternoon, and then tomorrow we can discuss details. In the meantime..." She winced again. "I'll need you to clean out your desk. This will be a remote position. But think of it this way," she added, flashing a thousand-watt smile that set Robyn's teeth on edge, "you'll have the kind of freedom a lot of people can only dream of."

"Thank you *very* much."

"You're welcome." Whether willfully or not, the sarcasm in Robyn's voice seemed to slip right over the editor-in-chief's head. As Robyn made for the door, her heart doing an angry tap dance in her chest, Melody called out, "And send Layla in, won't you?"

Robyn squeezed her eyes shut briefly, then wrenched open the door and marched out of Melody's office with her head held high, ignoring the whispers of her coworkers as she grabbed a box of printer paper, dumped its contents on the floor, and headed for her cubicle to begin packing up her things.

At least she had tonight to look forward to, she decided, throwing in a pack of pencils and a stapler with far more force than was necessary. Good things were coming her way.

And right now, she was so overwhelmed that she almost believed it.

CHAPTER 2

"So how was your day?" Keith asked, taking a generous sip of his wine as Robyn looked at the dessert menu without actually seeing it. She was too busy glancing covertly at Keith's pockets every chance she got, searching for the telltale bulge of a ring box—and she'd been doing that at least once every thirty seconds since he'd met her at the restaurant with a bouquet of orchids and a perfunctory kiss on the cheek.

Somewhere in the back of her mind, she was dimly aware of the hum of activity around her—the tuxedo-clad waiters speaking in hushed tones, the gentle clink of silverware and glasses as sumptuous meals were enjoyed, the romantic notes of violin music drifting over the diners' heads—but she was so laser-focused on Keith's every subtle move and tiny change in vocal inflection that she wasn't able to enjoy any of it.

Please, she thought. Please, please, please.

"My day was fine," she said, lifting her own glass of wine and feigning nonchalance. No way was she about to tell Keith the truth… not now. Not here. That could surely wait until tomorrow. Tonight was about them. It was about this moment. "Thank you again for the wonderful birthday dinner. I've been dying to try out Salvatore's for months, and it definitely didn't disappoint."

If she had been able to taste her food, that is. She *thought* she had ordered some type of pasta dish. She glanced down at the single smear of red sauce staining the white tablecloth and nodded to herself. Definitely pasta.

"So." A smile was playing at the corners of Keith's lips. "I'm sure you're excited to open your present." He reached into the inner pocket of his suit coat, and Robyn's breath caught.

This was it. The moment she'd been waiting for. Was it just her, or did the violin music choose that moment to swell? Almost as if it were playing for just the two of them.

Almost as if this were a romantic moment.

Happy marriages don't start out with an ultimatum.

There it was, that pesky thought again. Robyn worked hard to push it aside, forced herself instead to focus on Keith's hand, still rooting around in his pocket.

It wasn't as if they weren't happy. They were... as much as any other couple. Sure, they'd had their fair share of arguments, mostly about the future. More specifically, what Robyn wanted—no, *needed*—for the future, and what Keith had been unable, or unwilling, to give.

Commitment. A lifetime of it.

Was it his fault? That question had played in her mind countless times over the past few years, and she never could come up with a decisive answer.

He had come from a broken home. His parents' marriage was acrimonious, and the divorce that followed dragged on for years, with custody of their only son a back-and-forth battle of accusations and finger-pointing. When the dust finally settled, Keith had soured on the idea of marriage, a belief he had carried with him into adulthood. He loved her, he told her a year into their relationship. He would do anything for her.

Except *that*.

Robyn was the little girl who had put on elaborate wedding ceremonies with her stuffed animals, complete with white dresses and bouquets of wildflowers she'd picked in the woods behind her home. She was the teenager who'd dreamed of a Prince Charming who would swoop in and sweep her off her feet. She was the young woman with plans of a happy home and a family, complete with three bouncing babies and a dog who came when called and never chewed on the furniture. She was positive that someday she'd have a ring on that finger, an official piece of paper that spoke of the kind of love that lasted a lifetime.

So why had she stayed?

At first, she thought he would change his mind. That her love for him would conquer all of his fears and insecurities and the demons of his past. When she realized that it wasn't enough—that it would never *be* enough—she decided that she wanted him anyway, ring or no ring.

But somewhere along the way, things had changed. Perhaps she'd been a bridesmaid one too many times. Maybe she'd penned one too many articles on weddings and bliss and happily-ever-afters.

Or maybe she'd slowly begun to realize that if he found her worth it—really and truly worth it—he would have gotten down on one knee and promised himself to her long ago.

She was tired of being kept at arm's length. Embarrassed that the man she loved had an easy exit strategy, should things sour. No commitment? No problem.

The straw that broke the camel's back came one day when she least expected it. She and Layla were having dinner at a restaurant downtown, a much-needed girls' night that came around far too infrequently, when the man at the table next to them dropped to one knee, right in the middle of Robyn's last bite of chicken alfredo, and told his girlfriend—now fiancée—all the things she herself had always longed to hear.

Needless to say, the meal was ruined.

The ultimatum came the next day.

Propose by Robyn's next birthday, or she was leaving. This was *her* exit strategy, for once.

"I wasn't sure what to get you." Keith gave her that slow smile that had always made her go slightly weak in the knees as she leaned forward, her heart filled with anticipation, her eyes locked on his hand that was now emerging from his pocket. She could feel her breath catching, vaguely aware that the trio of strolling violinists were now standing directly beside their table.

No way was *that* a coincidence.

"Happy birthday, Robyn." Keith's voice was filled with sincerity. "I love you, and I hope you love this."

With that, he pushed an envelope across the table to her.

Robyn stared at it blankly for a few moments, ears ringing, blood rushing to her face—whether out of anger or embarrassment or grief or some combination of all three, she couldn't say. Her fingers were trembling like mad as she picked up the envelope, slit it open, and found herself staring at…

Concert tickets.

To a band she hadn't listened to in more than a decade.

"I know you've always liked them." Keith looked exceedingly pleased with himself. "So I've planned a whole night on the town—dinner, the concert, drinks… and a backstage meet-and-greet with the band. Autographs, photo opportunities, the whole nine yards." He took her hand; her fingers were numb. "You'll have an incredible time."

And then he picked up the dessert menu lying on the table between them and said, "I still have room for tiramisu. Don't you?"

Robyn didn't utter a word the entire car ride home, though Keith seemed not to notice the silence hanging heavily in the air between them. Instead, he told her a long, winding story about some client he had at the financial services firm where he worked. At least she thought he did. She wasn't listening.

Instead, she was staring out the window, her heart in her throat, wondering—*hoping*—that this was all an elaborate plan to trick her. Surely he had some romantic gesture planned, some swing-her-into-his-arms moment where he told her he was foolish to have waited all this time to ask her to be his wife.

Surely he understood that if he didn't, this was goodbye.

The tears blurred Robyn's vision as he turned onto their quiet street, and they were pouring down her cheeks as he parked the car in their driveway and yawned widely. "Man, I'm beat," he said, stretching his arms out toward the steering wheel and craning his neck from side to side. "I think I'll turn in early tonight. Unless you—"

He stopped speaking abruptly as she let out an involuntary sniffle, and before she could push open the car door, he was reaching for her, his eyes filled with concern. "Robyn, what's going on?"

"What's going on?" She stared at him in disbelief. "What's going *on*? *This* is what's going on." She whipped the envelope containing the concert tickets out of her purse and waved it in his face. "What is this?"

He ran one hand down his stubbled cheek, looking genuinely bewildered. "You don't like them?" Frowning, he added, "I can get you something else... I'm not sure about their refund policy but—"

By this point, she wasn't sure whether to laugh, cry, or hurl the envelope at his face. Instead, she spoke in as calm and measured a voice as she could muster. "What about... that thing I said about tonight? That if you didn't propose—"

"Oh, *that*?" Keith laughed, and Robyn was stunned to see that he looked relieved, as if this was a much easier problem to handle than unwanted concert tickets. "But you weren't serious about that." When her mouth actually dropped open in shock, he gave her a look that quite plainly said he thought she was being hysterical. "Why would you be? I told you, I'm not interested in marriage. You've known that from the start."

"You mean you're not interested in me." Robyn mopped at her eyes with the sleeve of her dress, the one she'd bought specially for the occasion. "If I were someone else—"

"Whoa." Keith held up his hands. "I don't *want* someone else." He shook his head. "You and I have been together for eight years, Robyn. We've built a life together." He waved his hand toward the house they shared. "If I wanted someone else, I would have been gone a long time ago."

"Ten years." The words came out as practically a whisper. "We've been together ten years."

"Okay." Keith raked his fingers roughly through his hair. "Eight years, ten years, does the number matter?"

"It does to me," Robyn snapped back. She turned to face him fully, forced herself to look into his eyes. "And what about the next ten years, Keith? Or the next thirty? Do you plan to stick with me until we're old and gray, or do you already have your suitcase packed and one foot out the door."

His face hardened, his expression becoming inscrutable. "I'm here now. Why are you suddenly worried about the future? Like I told you when we met, a piece of paper saying we're married means nothing to me. My parents had that, and look where it got them. By the time things ended, they could barely look at each other. Is that what you want?"

"I want love." Robyn turned and stared out the window at the darkening sky, the stars just beginning to twinkle above the treetops, the yellow moon that traced patterns across Keith's face in the car's dim interior. "I want someone who will promise himself to me forever. If you can't do that—"

"I can't." The words were sharp enough to force the breath from her lungs.

Robyn inhaled deeply, then patted her eyes dry one last time and gave him a resolute look. "Then I can't either."

And then she was opening the car door and slamming it closed, leaving Keith—and the echo of her words—alone in the darkness.

CHAPTER 3

*A*fter a sleepless night spent tossing and turning on the couch, and then mindlessly flicking through Netflix movies until the wee hours of the morning, Robyn rose, wrapped a robe around herself, and padded into the kitchen for a cup of coffee. As she sipped it, allowing the warmth to wrap around her like a soothing embrace, she gazed out the window at the first rays of the sun peeking over the horizon and strained to hear any sounds of movement coming from upstairs.

She hadn't spoken a word to Keith after storming into the house following her disastrous birthday dinner, choosing instead to lock herself in the guest bathroom and soak in the tub until the water grew tepid and the bubbles disappeared while considering her options for the future.

How quickly life had changed.

Job gone. Boyfriend gone. House? She glanced around the kitchen now, eyes roaming over the cheerful yellow décor she had chosen a few months after she'd moved in. At the time, she and Keith had just begun to grow serious, and his two-bedroom bungalow on a beautiful tree-lined street had looked far more appealing than the one-bedroom apartment she'd been renting near her downtown office. So she had traded her short commute time for suburban bliss and a sprawling backyard complete with swimming pool and veranda, whose shade she loved to read under on lazy summer days when she lounged barefoot with a glass of lemonade while Keith tended to his beloved vegetable garden nearby. Even though she had contributed her fair share to the bills, the house was—and would remain—his.

So now she could add homeless to the list too.

Suddenly, the coffee tasted bitter, and the formerly cheerful kitchen looked like a prison.

Robyn set down her mug and took a deep, steadying breath, hands braced against the counter, knuckles going white from the tension, before she straightened up, cinched her robe tighter around her waist, and padded into the small office off the kitchen. She made a beeline for the computer and switched it on, fingers drumming a nervous pattern on the desktop as she waited for the home screen to appear.

Right now, Robyn was a woman in crisis. And whenever life threw her a curveball, what did she do? Look for order. Make lists. Develop a plan for moving forward.

Step one, she decided, was to find a new job, something to supplement whatever meager income she would earn from her freelancing gig with Coastal Publications. Only then would she be able to look for a new living situation with confidence; in the meantime, she would live with... her sister?

Ugh. Perish the thought.

She loved Claire, and their bond of sisterhood ran deep, but they had never quite seen eye to eye on life in general. A few days—no, a *single* day—of living together would probably drive both of them to the brink of a breakdown.

That left only one other option: her father. Paul Wright was close to eighty but could easily pass for twenty years younger, and it was no secret that he missed having a houseful of women, especially since Robyn and Claire's mother had died many years ago.

The sprawling Victorian-style home she'd grown up in would be a welcome respite for Robyn while she nursed her broken heart and searched for a path forward in life, and she could quiet her unease over being over forty and still living with her father by reminding herself it was only temporary. A few weeks, at the most.

After that, freedom, and the single life—whether she was ready for it or not.

Feeling the weight on her shoulders lift slightly, allowing room for Robyn to breathe again, she searched the pocket of her robe for her cell phone and dialed the familiar number, balancing the phone between ear and shoulder as she opened a blank webpage and typed a few job-related keywords into the search bar. Her father answered as the computer churned out the search results, his voice robust and booming over the line despite the early hour.

"How's my little bird?"

Robyn smiled at the nickname and blinked back the tears threatening to form. "Hi, Dad," she said, managing to conceal the hoarseness of her voice—a result of the hours she'd spent crying alone in the darkness. "I'm okay… and you?"

"Better than ever. Listen, I'm glad you called—can you come over for brunch this morning? Claire too. And Keith, if he's available. I've got some news for all of you, and it's best served with homemade blueberry pancakes dripping with butter and maple syrup."

Robyn laughed and leaned back in the computer chair, enjoying a reprieve—however brief—from the sadness welling inside her. "How can I refuse an offer like that? And now that you've got my full attention, what kind of news are we talking? Good or bad? Because if I remember correctly, you've used your blueberry pancakes to deliver both."

"True, true." She could almost hear her father smiling down the line, could almost see the legendary twinkle in his ocean-blue eyes that had captivated her since she was a child. "But today is all good news, little bird. I'll tell you more when you get here... Hey," he said, as if realizing for the first time that he wasn't accustomed to receiving pre-dawn calls from his oldest daughter, "are you sure everything's okay? Shouldn't you still be in bed sleeping off whatever birthday festivities Keith planned for you last night?" He paused. "He *did* remember, didn't he?"

"Of course he did." Robyn cast her eyes to the ceiling, knowing from the telltale creak of the upstairs floorboards that her... whatever he was to her now... had risen. "I was just missing you, that's all, and thought I'd catch you for a quick chat before you went on your morning walk. I'll see you later, okay? What time do you want me there?"

"Eleven o'clock sharp. And pick up that sister of yours on the way. I have a feeling she'll want to hear this too."

Robyn said goodbye and ended the call, her temporary lift in spirits evaporating as she stared down at the silent phone. Whatever grand plans she'd had about returning home to lick her wounds would have to wait; no way was she going to ruin whatever news her father had with her own troubles. She glanced at the desk clock, noting that she could fit in a few more hours of job searching before she picked up her sister, then tapped out a quick text message to Claire informing her of the family brunch.

Despite her father's invitation, Keith wouldn't be attending.

She listened to the sounds of Keith moving upstairs, opening and closing the hallway closet before slipping into the bathroom and turning on the shower. Thankful that a few minutes remained before they would have to face each other, and endure whatever excruciating conversation awaited them, Robyn turned her attention back to the computer, quickly clicking through the job postings that populated the screen.

As expected, writing jobs were scant, and mostly aimed at college interns looking to add lines to their resume. When she changed her search to include part-time local listings in every category, deciding that a temporary gig doing anything was better than none at all, she scrolled mindlessly through the rows of unappealing-sounding jobs until one at the very bottom of the page caught her eye.

Wanted: part-time companion to elderly woman. Light housekeeping, assistance with daily activities and transportation, meal preparation, and other related activities. Must be willing to live full-time on Thistle Island. Room and board provided. Salary negotiable.

The listing included a telephone number to call for more information, and without realizing what she was doing, Robyn had pulled a pen and notepad out of the topmost desk drawer and scribbled it down, then stared at the numbers until they blurred on the page.

Thistle Island. She had been there only once as a child, but she clearly remembered the serenity she'd felt the moment she'd arrived on the small island off the coast that was the stuff of daydreams.

Dramatic, sweeping coastlines. Rugged, forested mountains. Sand so soft you could sink your feet in up to the ankles. And a friendly, welcoming community of year-round residents who took pride in their home.

It was also only an hour away by car… inconvenient without being burdensome when she wanted to visit family and friends. And with no job to tie her down…

It just might be the perfect escape.

"Robyn? Can we talk?"

Robyn jumped a little at the sound of Keith's voice, and only then did she register his presence in the doorway. Steeling herself, she set down the notepad and turned to face him—and was surprised to see that he looked like he'd gotten about as much sleep as she had last night.

"I'm not sure there's much to talk about." Robyn's voice remained resolute even though on the inside she felt like she was falling apart. His eyes were sunken, his cheeks hollow… was he reconsidering?

And did it even matter?

Keith ran his hands through his hair, then cupped them around his mouth for a moment as his eyes searched her face. "Can you just answer one question for me, then?" When she nodded, albeit reluctantly, he said, "Why does it have to be all or nothing?"

Robyn gave him a sad smile, one that was filled with regret for all the things they would lose. For all the things *he* would lose, because she was a good woman, and she loved him.

"Because I deserve all of you. Everything. And you've never given it to me. And Keith..." By now, her voice was barely a whisper. "I've had enough."

He nodded once, swallowing hard, his Adam's apple bobbing. "So what now?"

"Now I find a place to stay, and we put some distance between us." The words were more painful than she'd imagined; she felt as though her heart were splitting in two. How could the last ten years of her life have amounted to this?

To nothing.

"You don't have to leave right away, you know," Keith said, hands in the pockets of his flannel pajama pants as he studied her from the doorway. "I'm not going to kick you out." He gave her a small smile, one that was filled with something that looked a lot like hope. Like she would reconsider. Like this was a blip on the radar, something that would be remembered in years to come as inconsequential.

But Robyn knew better. It was a fork in the road,

and this time, she was taking the path she should have taken long ago.

"I'll be out by Monday," she said, and then turned her back on him, shoulders hunched, breath coming out in quick, sharp bursts until finally, she heard him quietly walk away.

∼

"So what do you think this is all about?" Claire asked as she slid into Robyn's car and buckled her seatbelt. "And thanks for waking me up at the crack of dawn, by the way. Nothing better to shoot you out of a dream about Ryan Gosling than your sister texting you at six a.m."

She turned a bright smile on Robyn, who automatically smiled back. Claire was her younger sister by five years, and she was the opposite of Robyn in every way—blonde hair to her brown, light eyes to her dark, feisty spirit to Robyn's more subdued outlook on life. Whereas Robyn had known from the time she was a child that she wanted to write for a living, Claire had drifted from job to job like a sailboat lost at sea, never staying in one place long enough, always looking for the next opportunity. She had approached her relationships in much the

THE HARBOR HOUSE

same way, and although she was loath to discuss it, Robyn had a feeling that she'd left a trail of broken hearts in her wake.

She hadn't always been so rudderless. When their mother had died, Robyn was twenty, but Claire was only fifteen, still navigating her way through the landmine that was teenagerhood, not yet blossoming into the woman she would become. Robyn still remembered—and still had nightmares about—the night the police officer knocked on their door to inform them, his eyes heavy with sadness, about the car accident that had claimed her life.

Her father had moved through the next few years of life robotically, barely taking care of himself but doing everything he could to keep his daughters in one piece. While Robyn had turned her grief inward, buckling down at her college studies and earning top marks in each class, Claire had become reckless, a daredevil, stealing their father's car in the middle of the night to go drag racing, or breaking into abandoned buildings with a group of kids just as lost as she was.

"I have no idea what Dad wants to tell us," Robyn said as she steered the car back onto the street and began the short drive to their childhood home. "But he sounded pretty excited."

"Do you think he's dating again?" Claire turned wide eyes on her sister. "If he and Mrs. Sinclair get together, I will absolutely die from the adorableness."

Mrs. Sinclair, the widow who had moved into the neighboring house a few years back, had an obvious crush on Paul Wright, laughing just a little too loudly while waxing poetic about her begonias, fluttering her eyelashes just a little too quickly whenever they discussed whose turn it was to mow the shared strip of lawn between their two driveways.

"Are you kidding me?" Robyn gave her sister a dubious look. "Mrs. Sinclair has to be, like, fifty-five. She's *way* too young for Dad."

"Oh, Robyn, can't you ever open your mind a little?" Claire shook her head and then reached forward to fiddle with the radio, flipping through the stations until she arrived at a country music one. "Love is love is love—who cares about age?" She bobbed her head in time to the music for a few seconds, then turned a wry smile on Robyn. "And speaking of love, how's my good friend Keith doing? Finally manning up and popping the question?"

She didn't bother hiding her disdain for Robyn's boyfriend, and who was Robyn to argue with that? Especially given the events of the past day. But she'd kept mum on the engagement ultimatum she'd issued for this very reason, and even now, she had no plans of telling her younger sister the truth. Claire had been harping on her for years to find someone who would give Robyn everything she wanted, and she'd only be too happy to find out that Robyn was finally planning to walk away.

"He's fine," she said in a casual voice. "Back at home doing something for work, but he said to give Dad his best."

Claire made a noncommittal sound that fell somewhere between a grunt and a snort, and they passed the rest of the drive in silence, save for the music blasting out of the radio, which her sister kept nudging higher and higher until Robyn felt like her eardrums would explode. When they finally arrived at their father's house—and waved to Mrs. Sinclair, who was out on her front lawn, no doubt waiting for Paul to step outside to grab his morning paper—they knocked on the front door and waited for him to greet them with one of his famous bear hugs.

Thankfully, he didn't disappoint, and after squeezing Claire to within half an inch of her life, he set his sights on Robyn, who was only too grateful to be enveloped in his comforting embrace. Fighting back tears, she breathed in his familiar musk-and-vanilla scent and for a brief moment, felt at peace.

"You're just in time," he said as he released Robyn and beckoned the girls to follow him to the dining room. "I've got the last of the pancakes on the griddle now, and if you'll allow me a moment to compliment myself, this batch is nothing short of superb."

He winked at the girls, then pulled out two chairs at the antique oak wood dining table their mother had inherited from her own mother before he disappeared back into the kitchen. The table was set with their mother's favorite linens, a cheerful blue-and-white checkered pattern that felt out of place given Robyn's low spirits.

She did her best to push past them, though, as she settled into her chair and draped the napkin over her lap. Only when Claire gave her a wink and a nudge did she realize that instead of the usual three place settings, a fourth had been added. *Mrs. Sinclair*, her sister mouthed with a knowing smile.

"Thanks, sweetheart, you've been a big help." Paul Wright's voice floated out from the kitchen, and a female one answered, her words muffled by the wall separating them, but the flirtatious tone was unmistakable. Robyn turned and looked out the window, frowning as she saw Mrs. Sinclair still kneeling in her garden, every so often shooting hopeful glances at Paul's front door. Then she turned back to Claire, and the sisters shared an excited look.

They had always encouraged their father to date, had urged him for years to find a companion. It was what their mother would have wanted, they told him. But he had always demurred, or changed the subject, or outright scolded them for meddling in matters that didn't concern them. His words, not theirs.

But now... it seemed like those matters had changed.

"Homemade blueberry pancakes, coming right up!" their father announced as he strode into the room with an enormous tray of pancakes and an equally enormous grin. "And don't think for one second that I forgot the syrup. My beautiful helper here has it all ready for you."

The sisters craned their necks to see past their father to the woman who was emerging from the kitchen after him. "Dad," Claire began in a mock-admonishing tone, "you didn't tell us you—"

But the rest of the words died on her lips as the woman came fully into view.

She had long blonde hair, wide blue eyes, porcelain skin, and a petite, trim figure. She was also at least fifteen years Robyn's junior—she pegged her for late twenties, at the very oldest. Early twenties if Paul wanted to give both daughters twin on-the-spot heart attacks.

"Hi," the woman said with a shy smile as she set the tureen of syrup on the table and walked over to stand beside Paul. He slipped his arm around her and pulled her to his side, gazing down on her with a look of pure adoration that had a bubble of rage forming in the pit of Robyn's stomach. "I've heard so much about you both that I feel like we've known each other for ages," she went on. "You must be Claire. And Robyn." She waved to each of them in turn. "I'm Jessica, but you can call me Jessie."

"Girls, I want to thank you," Paul chimed in, tightening his arm around Jessie's waist. "You've been telling me for years that I've got to put myself out there, and I finally decided that you were right. That very day, I went to the same coffee shop I've been going to for twenty years for my morning muffin and espresso, and I was fortunate enough to sit down right next to the most beautiful girl this old man has ever laid eyes on."

Claire made a strangled sound that she immediately turned into a hacking cough, while Robyn

THE HARBOR HOUSE

could do little else but stare, wide-eyed, from this, this... *child*... to her father and back again.

"And one more thing." Paul's eyes were shining with happiness. "The reason I brought you here today is not only because I wanted you to meet Jessica. It's because I wanted to tell you that we're engaged to be married."

"You've *got* to be kidding me." The words were out of Robyn's mouth before she could stop them—if she wanted to stop them, that is. Which, right now, she had no intentions of doing. She turned to her sister. "Are we living in the twilight zone? Is this one of those weird candid camera shows?" She glanced around the room, as if looking for confirmation, and when her eyes landed on her father's face, she saw that it was purple with barely suppressed rage.

"Jessie, sweetheart, please excuse me for a minute." To Robyn, he added in a clipped tone, "Come with me."

She threw down her napkin and followed him, barely registering that Claire was hot on her heels. Her father's back was ramrod-straight as he led them past the kitchen and out onto the attached patio that overlooked the house's expansive back lawn. In the distance, Mrs. Sinclair perked up, setting down her gardening trowel and patting her hair back into place.

"Robyn Lynn Wright, what is the *meaning* of this?" Paul's ocean-blue eyes were practically sparking with fury. "Your mother and I didn't raise you to be rude, especially to a guest in our home. In *my* home," he corrected. "What would she think if she could see you now?"

"What would she think if she could see *you* now?" Claire let out a soft gasp at Robyn's words, but she refused to back down. "That woman is young enough to be your granddaughter. What are you *thinking*? She's obviously a... a... *gold*-digger. You're lonely, and well-off, and she spotted an opportunity. She's playing you for a fool, Daddy."

By now, Robyn's lip was curled up in a snarl, her hands balled into fists at her sides, her eyes welling with tears of anger that she didn't bother brushing away. How *dare* this woman take advantage of her father. How dare she make him believe that she loved him. How dare she use an old man's loneliness to her own advantage. It was sick. It was twisted. And Robyn would move heaven and earth to make sure he didn't fall for it.

She opened her mouth again, but her father cut her off with a withering look and a slice of his hand through the air, both of which were enough to stop Robyn in her tracks. She might be over forty, but she was still Paul's daughter, and he commanded respect. Beside her, Claire rocked uncomfortably on the balls of her feet, her gaze every so often wandering into the house as if to make sure that Jessie wasn't listening.

Robyn fervently hoped she was.

"Enough." Paul's voice was heavy with disappointment. "You've said your piece, but I won't hear another word against Jessica. She's a wonderful woman, and she doesn't deserve any of the things you've said about her. You don't even know her." He leaned against the porch railing, his weathered hands gripping the white-painted wood as he stared out over the backyard, toward the weeping willow tree that had been a favorite reading spot of Robyn's mother.

"I'm tired of being alone," he murmured, "and I've spent far too long mourning the loss of the woman who meant everything to me. Jessie has brought new light into my life, and she's rekindled something in my heart that I didn't even know was possible after all these years. I didn't bring you here to ask your permission—she and I are going to be married with or without you. I brought you here so you could meet her and share in my joy. Since you can't do that right now, I'm asking you to leave. This is a special moment for us, and I won't have it ruined."

Robyn stared hard at her father. "You're choosing her over me?"

Paul Wright cocked his head, regarding his oldest daughter with a mild expression that didn't belie the sadness in his eyes. "I never asked to be making a choice. You're forcing my hand, and you're in the wrong. Until you've come to your senses, you're not welcome here. When you're ready to apologize to Jessie and get to know her without making assumptions and harsh judgments, then my door will be open." He turned back to the house, opening the porch door and letting it bang shut behind him.

Robyn watched him go, her cheeks red with anger, her heartbeat pounding in her ears.

Claire put a hand on her shoulder. "Maybe we should give her a—"

"Because love is love is *love*, right, Claire?" She made no attempt at hiding the disgust in her tone. "You can't tell me you're happy about this—she doesn't *love* him. She's using him."

"Maybe so." Claire's voice was quiet, barely above a whisper. "But if that does turn out to be the case, don't you think he's going to need us now more than ever?"

Robyn swallowed hard, pushing down a fresh wave of tears, and turned a stormy gaze on her younger sister. "He asked me to leave, so I'm leaving. Are you coming with me?"

Claire's eyes drifted toward the house, her expression torn. She opened her mouth to speak and then closed it again with a shake of her head, which was all the confirmation Robyn needed. Without another word, she took the porch stairs two at a time and made a beeline for her car, driving down the street without a backward glance at the Victorian house—and the father—she loved so much.

She wouldn't stand by and watch his heart break. She couldn't. Not when her own heart was also torn in two.

As she drove, Robyn reviewed the events of the past twenty-four hours and wondered when her life had taken such a deep dive into the abyss.

No job. No boyfriend. And now, no place to go or family members to lean on.

In between those thoughts, others crept in too, burrowing into her mind and refusing to let go.

Pristine beaches that stretched for miles. The

white flash of seagulls against a crystalline sky. Air so clean you could practically bathe in it.

By the time she reached home, her next steps were clear.

Change awaited her. A new beginning. A chance to start fresh.

Ignoring Keith, who tried to intercept her as she headed through the house, she reached the office and switched on the computer, then reread the job posting a final time and gazed down at the telephone number she'd written down earlier. Then, taking a deep breath, she squared her shoulders, picked up her phone, and began to dial.

CHAPTER 4

This is crazy. You're moving to Thistle Island? You barely wanted to leave the city and come live with me in the suburbs when we met. Come on, Robyn, you don't really want this. Let's sit down and work this out.

"There's nothing to work out," Robyn said to herself as she rolled down the window and let the fresh, early-morning summer air sweep into the car, instantly boosting her mood and wiping out Keith's words as he watched her load her suitcase into the trunk before setting off. He'd insisted on staying home from work to see her off, and as much as the gesture irritated Robyn, the look of deep sadness on his face had been one she'd been unable to shake off.

Leaving him was hard. Devastating, really. But what other choice did she have?

As she drove through the winding streets of her former neighborhood on her way to the highway that would take her toward the coast, and beyond it, her new home, Robyn reflected on what it would mean to leave Keith behind, once and for all. Could she truly do it? Even now she longed to call him, to admit that a small part of her wondered whether she was making a mistake.

He was a good man, and good men were hard to come by, especially at this stage of her life. Why was she so focused on marriage, anyway? He'd been committed—had proven that to her for the past decade. So what was her reason for focusing so much on that next step?

Because she was worth it, she reminded herself. She was worth a commitment not just now, not just for the next ten years, but for a lifetime and beyond. She was worth someone telling her that she was the only one for him. If she compromised, if she continued to settle, she would be compromising her own self-worth, too. And that was something she could no longer live with.

But that didn't mean her pain was any less all-consuming. It didn't mean the doubts weren't constantly pushing their way to the forefront of her mind. Or that she sometimes had to physically stop herself from taking the next exit and heading for home.

For him.

"I hope I'm doing the right thing," she whispered as the coastline finally came into view. The day was promising to be a magnificent one, with a cloudless sky that seemed to stretch endlessly over the houses that dotted the shoreline. Plenty of people were enjoying the sunshine today, she noted, gazing wistfully at a woman sitting alone by the shoreline, digging her toes into the water-drenched sand as she buried her head in a book, wide-brimmed hat shielding her from the sun's unforgiving glare.

Then Robyn reminded herself that she had no reason to be jealous of this woman. Soon, she too would be soaking in the sand and sea. At least that's what the woman at the hiring agency had assured her of during her interview. According to her, Robyn's new job as a companion would be relatively low-key, with plenty of time for work-life balance and other pursuits. The elderly woman, Helen Moore, was hesitant about letting someone into her home, but her nephew, who lived next door and contacted the agency in the first place, insisted that she needed help. After a fall had sent her to the hospital, Helen had reluctantly agreed.

Robyn was nervous about meeting Helen, worried that perhaps she wasn't the right fit for this type of work. After all, her journalism background didn't exactly lend itself to a caretaking position, and Keith's warnings—and her own fears—that she was being impulsive, that she was running away from her problems instead of facing them head-on, didn't help her misgivings.

Over the past few days, she had picked up the phone at least a dozen times to contact the hiring agency and withdraw her name from consideration. The last time that had happened, the phone had rung in her hand before she could work up the nerve to dial.

The job was hers. Effective immediately. Did she still want it?

In that moment, not a single hesitation entered Robyn's mind. The answer was a resounding yes.

The bridge that connected Thistle Island to the mainland came into view, its steel columns glittering invitingly in the sunshine. Only a single car traversed it, which wasn't unexpected. The local leaders had worked hard to preserve Thistle Island's natural beauty, and the small community who lived and worked there year-round. No hotels or resorts were permitted to take up residence on the island, which meant that summer-vacationers had to content themselves with day trips to enjoy Thistle Island's scenic wonder. Whereas the beaches up and down the coastal mainland were already packed with tourists, even at this early hour, the island's shores would be quiet, restful, an almost unheard-of respite from the outside world.

It was everything Robyn needed.

As she turned onto the bridge, Robyn let out the breath she hadn't realized she'd been holding and did her best to concentrate on the drive while reveling in the beauty surrounding her. The ocean was deep blue and rippling with gentle white-capped waves, a seagull dipped in and out of the lone cloud hovering over the water, its wings tipped in sunshine, and a cluster of small fishing boats bobbed on the horizon, searching for the day's catch.

The island stretched before her in all its glory, its forested mountains forming a dramatic backdrop to the shimmering shoreline. Small, colorful bungalows and cottages were nestled in the valley below the mountains, and houses raised on stilts sat closer to the sea.

This, Robyn decided, her eyes brimming with unexpected tears, was nothing short of paradise.

She reached the end of the bridge and navigated her car onto the tight two-lane road that led to a guardhouse situated at the edge of the island, rolling down her window to greet the guard, a middle-aged man with a sun-bronzed face and warm brown eyes.

"Hello there," he said jovially, leaning out of his station to greet her. "Do you need a visitor pass for the day? You'll need one to access the national park and any historic sites you might be planning on visiting. Camping overnight is permitted, but you'll need to speak with the ranger about that. His name is—"

Robyn stopped his monologue with a shake of her head, not wanting to waste the man's time. "I'm actually here to start a new job."

"New job?" The guard frowned and scratched idly at his chin. "Didn't realize any of the businesses were hiring."

Then he chuckled when he saw the look of surprise on her face. "That probably sounds like an odd thing to say, huh? But with a place as small as Thistle Island, everybody knows everybody else—and everybody else's business, too. Personal business, that is," he added with a wink. "Not the money-making kind." Then he laughed again. "Well, that too, I suppose, given that I don't know what job you're talking about."

Robyn laughed too, deciding instantly that she liked this man. "It's a companion position," she said, one elbow on her rolled-down window as she smiled up at him. "For a woman by the name of Helen Moore?"

"Oh, Helen, she's a real treat." The guard shook his head, grinning. "Ninety-eight years old and spunky as all else. But her health hasn't been the best recently, so I suppose it's only natural that she'd need someone to help her out around the house. Her nephew, Levi, and his little girl live next door, and do what they can to help out, but he's got his hands full too. Helen's always been a bit on the private side, though, so I'm not surprised to hear that she didn't broadcast the news that she was looking to hire a caretaker." He gave Robyn an appraising look. "You seem like a nice lady. Welcome to Thistle Island. Have you been here before?"

"Once, as a child," she said, gazing once more at the forested mountains rising above the ocean. "Only for a day, but it made a big impression. I've been looking to make a change in my life, and when

I saw the job posting, I applied on a whim—I didn't think I'd actually get it."

She smiled up at him once more, surprised that she was sharing so much with a man she'd known all of two minutes. But his eyes were kind and his smile was welcoming, and she could use a friend—especially now.

"I expect not too many people would be willing to move to an island as small as this one, but between you and me, they're missing out. That's the beauty of Thistle Island, though—we keep a tightknit community, and we're glad to be off the map."

Just then, another car pulled off the bridge and sat idling behind Robyn. "Well, duty calls," the guard said, tipping his hat to Robyn. "I'm glad to meet you. Name's Garrett, by the way."

"I'm Robyn. Before I go, would you mind pointing me toward Helen's house? The directions I got were a little fuzzy, and my GPS has been going haywire since I got on the bridge. At one point it told me to take a right turn clear into the ocean."

Garrett chuckled. "Told you we're off the map. And I'd be glad to. Helen and Levi both live on the harbor—you can't miss it, just follow the coastal road to the other side of the island. You'll see a big

THE HARBOR HOUSE

dock where a bunch of ships are moored. Helen's house is the yellow one with the white trim, and Levi has the green one right next door to her."

Glancing in her rearview mirror, Robyn could see that the occupants of the car behind her were looking mildly impatient at the holdup, so without further ado, she thanked Garrett for his help and entered the island proper. She turned right onto the coastal road and rolled down the passenger window too, enjoying the fresh saltwater breeze that blew through the car. The road was nearly empty at this time of the morning, and the small shops and eateries that lined it were still mostly shuttered.

She drove by a café that was doing a brisk business; its rows of outdoor tables shaded by cheerful yellow and blue umbrellas were filled with diners. A couple of people were taking early-morning strolls on the beach across from the café, and a mother and father and their three young children were hunting for seashells in the sand, buckets at their side. The sun was already blazing down on the island, promising a perfect summer day.

The island was small, so it didn't take long for Robyn to reach the other side. As Garrett had promised, she found the harbor easily, and took a moment to enjoy the sight of the boats, both recreational and commercial, bobbing in the gentle waves. A small cluster of houses overlooked the harbor, each painted in a bright pastel color, and Robyn immediately spotted a small yellow bungalow with a wide front patio that overlooked the shimmering water. The house's front yard was small but tidy, with rows of beautiful rose bushes lining the walkway in every color imaginable. The front door was adorned with a cheerful wreath made of ivy and baby's breath, and two Adirondack chairs were positioned on either side of it overlooking the harbor, each with a small side table perfect for holding a book or a glass of lemonade.

Robyn found a parking space in front of the pier that jutted out into the water and exited her car, leaning against the door for a moment as she gazed up at the house, her heart in her throat, keenly aware that this beautiful place represented the new beginning that she had been searching for. The change she so desperately needed.

"Here goes nothing," she whispered to herself, then crossed the road and strode up the cobblestone pathway to the bungalow's front door. She knocked twice, then stepped back, turning to admire the view from the porch while she waited for someone to answer.

THE HARBOR HOUSE

She didn't have to wait long—barely ten seconds had passed before the door was flung open and a diminutive woman with wild white hair and turquoise glasses stood in the threshold, beaming at her. "You must be the new servant," she said, eyeing Robyn up and down with her arms folded. "I suppose you'll do, but I'm warning you, this job isn't going to be easy—I hear the boss is a real pain in the you-know-what." Then, faded blue eyes sparkling with laughter, she waved her hand in the air and said, "I kid, I kid. She's only a pain half the time. The other half, she's a real riot." She extended her hand to Robyn. "I'm Helen."

Robyn had to work hard to keep her jaw from dropping open in shock as they shook hands. *This* was Helen? The woman seemed sprier than Robyn herself, and young enough to pass for her father's age. If this was ninety-eight, then Robyn wanted every part of it.

"I'll try not to be too offended by that look of surprise on your face," Helen said, her eyes still twinkling with laughter. "Thanks to the help-wanted ad my nephew put out, you were probably expecting someone who was practically bedridden. He's a good boy, but a little too much of a fusspot, if you ask me. His heart's in the right place, though, and after that little tumble I took, any arguments I tried to make that I was perfectly fine on my own went right out the window."

She stepped back and beckoned Robyn inside. "What are you waiting for? It's about time that you see what you've gotten yourself into." As Robyn stepped into the small foyer, she added, "I took the liberty of having some breakfast delivered for your first day. I figured we could sit out on the porch, have a few bites, and get to know one another."

"That sounds wonderful," Robyn said, feeling instantly at ease in the older woman's presence—and suddenly unable to keep the grin off her face.

The feeling of excitement—and *rightness*—she was experiencing only increased as Helen showed her around the small but well-kept home, which included a cheerful breakfast nook with a small, two-person table and chair set, a window-enclosed back room with comfortable-looking cushioned wicker furniture, and a bright and airy bedroom that overlooked the harbor. Only when Helen finished their short tour of the house did Robyn realize that something was missing—something big.

"My apologies if I've gotten the details wrong," she said, frowning slightly, "but I was under the impression that this was a live-in position. The ad said room and board are included, but I don't see a second bedroom." She didn't want to add that if it wasn't included, she'd have to take up residence somewhere under the pier alongside the seagulls and beached fish, but her tone must have betrayed her anxiety, because the older woman gave her a sincere smile.

"Don't worry, I promise you'll be thrilled with your living quarters." She gestured out the window, toward the house next door. "My nephew, Levi, has a space all ready for you. To tell you the truth, he's my great-nephew—my younger sister's grandson, God rest her soul. But I like to pretend to be much younger than I really am. Delaney can't wait to meet you, either—that's his little girl. She's a doll, comes around whenever she can to help me out. Makes things harder for me sometimes, but she can't help it —she's only seven." Helen chuckled fondly.

This time, Robyn didn't smile back. "Your nephew's house?" She glanced out the window at the larger house next door, not bothering to hide her discomfort. This Levi, whoever he was, was a perfect stranger to Robyn—and sure, Helen could make the same argument about herself, but Robyn knew that despite the old woman's spunk, she'd have no trouble fending her off with a baseball bat.

Not that she was planning to do that to either of them, of course, but a strange man in a strange house inspired all sorts of true-crime images to pop into her head.

"Now don't you worry about your privacy," Helen said, watching Robyn with amusement. "Any woman would be an idiot to move in with a man she's never met, and I don't hire idiots to work for me. Levi has a detached guest house behind his home that he's been renting out for years. It's been unoccupied for a while now, so it'll be no trouble for you to stay there. It has a private entrance and plenty of locks on the doors and windows." At those last words, she winked, and Robyn could feel herself coloring.

"I'm sorry, I didn't mean to imply—"

"You're sorry for nothing, and you didn't imply anything at all." Helen waved away her words as she gestured for Robyn to follow her into the living room, where they took seats opposite each other on the couch. "A woman has to be smart, especially these days. Besides, you won't be seeing much of Levi. The man keeps to himself as much as he can. Been that way since Sara died, God rest her soul."

"Who's—" Robyn began to ask, but was interrupted by a knock on the door.

"Thank the heavens, that'll be our breakfast." Helen was on her feet faster than Robyn, leading her to once again wonder just which one of them actually needed the caretaker. After accepting an enormous paper bag from a teenage delivery boy with sun-kissed skin and a shirt that said *The Beachcomber Café*, Helen carried it into the kitchen and started unloading Styrofoam containers and plastic-wrapped silverware.

"Here, let me." Robyn gently nudged her aside and took her place at the counter, inhaling the delicious aroma of breakfast foods wafting out from the bag.

"Thanks." Helen pulled a chair out from the kitchen table, and Robyn noticed she was gripping the armrests tightly as she slowly lowered herself into it. "I've been on my own for so many years that I have no idea how to accept help. I have to warn you, this new arrangement of ours is going to be a challenge for me." She gave Robyn an appraising look. "But I think we're going to get along just fine. You have a kind face, and that tells me all I need to know about you."

As Robyn found two plates in the cabinet and dished out a delicious-looking breakfast of scrambled eggs, bacon, strawberry muffins, French toast, and freshly squeezed grapefruit juice for each of them, Helen asked her a few basic questions about herself, and answered a few of her own.

"Never been married," she said as Robyn hunted around in the refrigerator for a bottle of syrup and some salsa for the eggs that Helen had requested. "And I'm guessing the same about you." She glanced at Robyn's bare ring finger, then nodded in confirmation. "But a pretty girl like you has at least one man hanging around her, hoping for a chance, I'm sure."

Keith's face flashed through her mind, though the accompanying pain was a little duller this time. "It's… complicated," she murmured. Then, in a much brighter voice, she announced, "Breakfast is ready! Should we eat in here?" She moved toward the small table, but Helen shook her head. If she noticed the abrupt change in topic, she made no mention of it.

"When the weather's this beautiful, I always enjoy my meals outside. Fresh air makes everything taste better."

Robyn happily agreed, and a few moments later, the two of them were seated at a pair of wicker chairs on the back patio with the most breathtaking mountain view that she had ever seen. Between that, and the gently rolling ocean behind them, Robyn had no idea which way to look. She was surrounded by paradise.

"Glorious, isn't it?" Helen said when she saw Robyn admiring the view. "I'm humble enough to know that I *don't* know a lot of things, but I do know this: Thistle Island is heaven on earth."

"Have you lived here your whole life?" Robyn asked as she used a knife to split her muffin in two and add a pat of butter to each side.

"Off and on." Helen bit into a crisp slice of bacon. "I spent some time in Europe when I was a much younger woman, but I always knew this was home."

Just then, the rumble of a truck engine broke the silence around them, and Helen glanced up from her plate. "Oh, look who it is." She jabbed her finger toward the pickup truck pulling into the driveway next door, then wiped her mouth with her napkin, set down her fork, and stood from the chair, motioning to Robyn with a smile. "The time has come for you to meet your warden. Otherwise known as my nephew, Levi Graham."

CHAPTER 5

*R*obyn followed Helen across the small lawn that separated her house from the one next door, arriving just in time to greet Levi as he descended from his pickup truck, paper bag of groceries tucked under his arm. Even though she didn't know anything about Helen's nephew—except, of course, that he was a loner and a fusspot, according to her—given that he chose to live year-round on an island, she'd pegged him for the surfer type: blond hair, blue eyes, cocky smile, and a tan that would last through the winter months.

And while that last part proved to be true, with his dark hair and eyes, rugged jawline, and days-old stubble, not to mention dirt-streaked jeans, button-down shirt with sleeves rolled up to the elbows, and wide-brimmed hat, he looked like he'd stepped off the cover of a Western novel. The scowl on his face didn't do much to detract from that observation either, Robyn noted, raising her eyebrows and taking an automatic step back from the truck just as Helen approached it, beaming.

"Look what the cat dragged in!" she said in a singsong voice, standing on her tiptoes to brush a kiss against Levi's cheek. The hard lines and planes of his face immediately softened at the sight of her, and he leaned back to scrutinize her.

"How are you feeling today? Did you take your blood pressure pills?"

"This man has always been quite the charmer," Helen said, turning to Robyn with a look of amusement. Then she patted his cheek lovingly. "But thanks for looking out for me, sweets." She peered into the passenger seat of the pickup. "Where's my Delaney girl?"

"She had a sleepover with a couple of her friends last night. I'm sure she'll want to run over and see you as soon as I pick her up." Levi set the bag of groceries down at his feet and leaned into the truck to hoist out another one. "Your refrigerator was looking a little bare when I stopped by yesterday, so I took the liberty of picking up a few things for you at the market." He shot Robyn a look that bordered on annoyance, as though she was somehow responsible for the state of her new charge's kitchen before she even started the job.

Helen peered into the first bag. "Did you get my ice cream and those barbecue chips I love so much?"

"No." Levi's mouth quirked, but he quickly suppressed the hint of a smile, replacing it instead with a stern look. "I got you fresh vegetables, some melon, and lean meat."

"Oh, phooey." Helen sighed, then turned back to Robyn with a morose expression. "See? I told you he was no fun. All work and no play makes Levi a grumpy boy."

"Very amusing." Levi leaned around his great-aunt and reached out a hand toward Robyn. "You must be Robyn Wright."

And that was it by way of introduction, Robyn thought as she shook his calloused hand. No *pleased to meet you*. No *welcome to the island*. No *did you find the house okay?*

No warmth. No laughter. No spunk.

He was the opposite of Helen in every way.

"I thought this would be the perfect time to show Robyn her new home," Helen said to Levi, and then beamed at Robyn. "Trust me, you're in for a real treat. Follow me." She bustled past the two of them, leading the way across the house's gravel driveway to a path lined with stepping stones that wound toward the backyard. Each stepping stone was hand-painted with colorful pictures of suns, trees, and in one case, a llama.

"Delaney does have a flair for the creative," Helen said when Robyn stopped to admire the stone. "The girl's never seen a llama in her life, though, so how she came up with that one, I'll never understand. For all we know, it's a horse gone wrong and we've been praising her for it all this time." She laughed softly. "That girl brings a lot of light into my life."

The backyard was recently mowed and well-kept, with the same dramatic mountainous backdrop that Robyn had enjoyed from Helen's patio. In addition to a vegetable and fruit garden bursting with life, the yard boasted a white trellis with climbing ivy, a charming wishing well, and a sitting area beneath a sprawling dogwood tree. At the back of the property, nestled in a grove of pine trees, was a small cottage with sea-green paint and whitewashed shutters. It was enclosed with a white picket fence, and a pair of Adirondack chairs identical to the ones on Helen's front porch sat beside the front door. A fountain in the shape of three leaping dolphins babbled softly from the small side yard next to an in-ground firepit lined with mismatched stones.

As she swept her eyes over every nook and cranny of the cottage, Robyn could barely contain her excitement. Any misgivings she'd had about living on Levi's property melted away as she set her hand on the gate, which swung open with a creak, and headed up the cobblestone walkway to the front door.

"It's something, isn't it?" Helen said, watching Robyn for a reaction. Levi stood nearby, his arms crossed over his chest, his expression unreadable.

"It's *amazing*," Robyn breathed. "Like something out of a magazine." Indeed, the picturesque harbor houses that Helen and Levi called home would easily be a featured story in *Coastal Designs*. Maybe she would pitch a two-page spread on Thistle Island as her first freelance assignment for her former employer. Robyn made a mental note to explore that idea further, then turned to Levi.

"May I take a look inside?"

With a nod, Levi dug around in the pocket of his jeans before producing a small, slightly battered silver key on a ring. "Be my guest. I'll leave you to it. If you have any questions, give me a knock. I'll be home for the next couple of hours catching up on some paperwork." Then he turned without another word and strode back to the front of the house.

Robyn stared after him for a moment in bemusement, then turned to Helen with a slight smile. "A man of few words, I see."

Helen sighed. "He wasn't always that way. Never the life of the party, mind you, but after his wife passed… well, he hasn't been the same since. Losing the love of your life will do that to you." Her sparkling eyes dimmed noticeably as she followed her nephew's progress toward the house. "Being a single father has been hard on him, but he's never uttered a word of complaint. He loves that little girl with all his heart, and he does his best every day by her." She shook her head. "Such a tragedy." Then she turned to Robyn with a gentle smile. "But enough sadness for one day. Why don't we take a look inside your new house?"

Robyn cast one last glance at Levi's retreating figure, noting the slight slouch to his walk and the way his hands were shoved deep into the pockets of his jeans, and then gazed down at the key in her hand. She hadn't had a place of her own in many years, and even though she had been mostly happy in the home she shared with Keith, this moment, right here, truly represented the first step in moving on.

Taking a deep breath, and then inwardly laughing at herself for being so nervous about entering a rental house, she slotted the key in the lock and pushed open the front door. Despite the towering pine trees that surrounded the bungalow, the interior was bathed in light. It was humble but cozy, with a small living room furnished with a comfortable-looking couch and recliner, a bright, airy kitchen painted pale yellow, and a bedroom perfect for one person, with a small gas fireplace tucked in one corner and a slightly motheaten comforter and curtain set in bright purple. Those she could easily fix, she decided, fingering a loose thread in the comforter before heading for the window. As she yanked open the curtains, her breath caught as she took in the view—sweeping pine trees climbing a mountain that rose high above her, so tall it seemed to brush up against the single puffy cloud floating lazily by.

"I know it doesn't have a harbor view," Helen said

from the doorway, causing Robyn to jump a little—she'd completely forgotten the older woman was even there. "But you're welcome to pull up a chair on my front porch anytime and watch the ships sail by. It's one of my very favorite pastimes."

"Thank you," Robyn said, turning to her and sweeping her arm around the room. "For all of this." Her voice caught on the last word, and she shook her head with a soft smile. "I really needed a change, and this... this is perfect."

Helen's eyes swept over her face for a moment, studying her, and when she spoke next, her voice was gentle with understanding. "Sometimes the heart needs time and space to heal from whatever is troubling it. Believe me when I say that there's no better place to do that than right here on Thistle Island. I have personal experience in the matter."

She stepped over to Robyn and placed a hand on her shoulder. "Why don't you take a few more minutes to look around. I'll wait outside, and then when you're done, I'd like to head back over to my place and finish our breakfast and our conversation." She gave Robyn's shoulder a light squeeze. "I'm looking forward to getting to know you."

Robyn smiled back at her, blinking back the tears that had unexpectedly formed. "Me too." She laughed and swiped at her eyes with the back of her hand. "I'm sorry—I have no idea why I'm getting so emotional. I feel silly reacting this way to a house."

"Because it's not about the house, my dear girl. It's about what the house represents—and that's something only you can look inside your heart and answer." Helen's grip on her shoulder tightened briefly, and then she released her hold on Robyn and padded from the room.

Exhaling softly, Robyn moved to the window once more and took a long moment to admire the view. Far overhead, a seagull swept through the sky, its wings catching the light, and a quiet breeze had lifted up from the ocean, swaying the pine trees' branches. She was just about to follow Helen out of the house when her phone buzzed in her pocket.

Sliding it out, she thumbed open the lock screen and stared down at the message waiting for her.

I miss you already. Please reconsider.

As if on autopilot, Robyn swiped up her keyboard to respond, her fingers hovering over the keys uncertainly.

I miss you too, she wanted to say. Because anything else would be a lie.

Then she stopped. Took a deep breath. And

quietly turned off the phone and slipped it back into her pocket.

She could sort out the mess her life had become another time.

Breakfast—and a conversation with a lovely new friend—awaited.

CHAPTER 6

*R*obyn spent the better part of the next couple of days exploring the island to familiarize herself with the layout of the town and helping Helen with basic tasks around the house. True to her word, the older woman had a hard time relinquishing control on the first day, but by the following morning, she had eased up, and each of them began to settle into their new role.

"I thought we could drive into town today and do some shopping," Helen said from her place at the kitchen table as she watched Robyn ladle blueberry pancake batter onto the griddle. She was a decent cook, though she'd never quite been able to replicate the fluffy, mouthwatering pancakes that her father prided himself on.

As she thought of her father, she felt a pang of sorrow in her chest, and automatically glanced at her phone on the counter. She'd never gone this many days without speaking to him, but he'd ordered her to keep her distance until she could find it in her heart to accept Jessie into their family.

And she couldn't do that. Not now. Maybe not ever.

Claire had sent her a couple of text messages over the past few days to check in, but Robyn had left them unanswered. The sting of her sister's rejection still hurt, and she wasn't ready to rehash the disastrous brunch at their father's house just yet.

She hadn't heard from Keith again.

"Shopping sounds great," Robyn said, flipping over a pancake. Seeing its perfect golden-brown color, she slid it onto a plate along with two others and passed it to Helen.

"You keep cooking this way and I'm going to need a whole new wardrobe," Helen said, reaching happily for the bottle of syrup and pouring enough of it on the pancakes to flood the plate. "I've been living mostly on boiled eggs and cheese sandwiches—when you're ninety-eight years old and have spent most of your life cooking for one, you just lose interest in it after a while and go for convenience."

"What about all those groceries that Levi buys for you?" Robyn turned from the griddle to frown at the older woman. "Fresh vegetables, fruits, meat…?" Just last night, at Helen's direction, she had prepared an enormous bowl of blackened chicken, peppers, and onions on the charcoal barbecue grill on the back deck; she'd assumed it was for tonight's dinner, with plenty of leftovers to enjoy for days.

Helen smiled mysteriously. "Let's just say they get put to good use. Which reminds me." She nodded toward the empty paper grocery bags, now folded and tucked in one corner of the kitchen. "Before we hit the town, we need to load up those bags and stop off at the beach. Lifeguard tower number three."

Robyn cocked her head at the odd request and then decided not to press—she'd find out what Helen was up to soon enough. "Sounds good to me," she said instead. "I haven't had a chance to see much of the beaches yet, and I've been dying to sink my feet into that golden sand." She slid into the chair across from Helen and reached for the syrup. "If we're going into town, would it be okay if we stopped for a few minutes at a linen store, or whatever equivalent you might have on the island? I need to pick up a new bedspread and curtains for the house."

The smile faded from Helen's face, and she set down her fork and leaned back in her chair. "New bedspread and curtains?" she repeated.

"Yes." Robyn looked at her curiously. "Is that okay? I can always venture out on my own later if—"

"No, no." Helen recovered, waving her hand in the air and shaking her head. "We'll have plenty of time. In fact, I know just the place."

Even though Robyn was puzzled by the older woman's initial reaction to her request, she shook it off, chalking it up to some sort of fleeting misunderstanding. They spent the rest of the breakfast chatting amicably, and as Helen returned to her bedroom to prepare for their drive into town, Robyn headed for her car to load up the meal she had cooked the previous night, along with the rest of the groceries Levi had dropped off for his great-aunt. A few minutes later, she was behind the wheel, Helen beside her, the fresh sea air tousling their hair as they drove down the coastal road that wound around the island.

Robyn had been surprised to discover that despite its quaintness, the town had a bustling main square, with enough shops, businesses, and eateries to keep the residents from having to make regular treks to the mainland. There were several entertainment options as well, including a movie theater that played all the latest releases, a small concert hall where local musicians and theater groups put on concerts and productions, and a bowling alley and arcade that attracted the younger crowd.

That was in addition to the outdoor activities available on Thistle Island—enough to keep Robyn's schedule filled during the times when she wasn't assisting Helen at home or around the town. There was a wildlife sanctuary and preserve that focused on protecting the island's native birds, a sprawling garden and park set high on a bluff overlooking the ocean, a historic lighthouse—one of the few along the eastern seaboard still in operation—and plenty of camping and recreation sites set aside for the residents' use. If she was ever feeling adventurous, Robyn could also take advantage of the many water sports and boating activities available on the island.

"So you've been here a few days now—what are your first impressions of the island?" Helen asked, raising her voice so Robyn could hear her above the wind.

"Glorious. Magical. Magnificent. An actual paradise on earth that most people are completely unaware of."

"And thank goodness for that." Helen adjusted

her turquoise glasses and grinned at Robyn. "I've lived in the big cities before and they just didn't do it for me. Too many people, too many cars, everybody looking right past you in their hurry to chase the next job opportunity, or try out the hottest new restaurant, or buy a house that's a few square feet bigger than their neighbors' houses. At the end of the day, that doesn't bring you happiness. *This* does." She trailed her hand out the window, letting the saltwater breeze blow through her fingers.

"I wish someone had told me that when I was just starting out on my own." Robyn brushed a few windblown strands of hair out of her mouth. "The focus was always getting ahead, getting ahead, getting ahead—and now, I'm starting to wonder… for what, exactly?"

She thought of the countless expensive nights out that she and Keith had enjoyed together and realized now that they all blurred together. But would she ever forget the smell of the breeze rolling in off the ocean when she stepped outside her new home every morning? Or the pillowy sand giving way beneath her feet as she scanned the shore for the pink seashells she'd already begun to collect in a vase on her bedside table?

Somehow, outside of her awareness, the island had already become ingrained in her very soul.

Robyn stopped her car at a crosswalk to allow a young couple strolling hand in hand to walk across the road toward the beach. Helen, who had just begun filling Robyn in on the finer points of the Thistle Island road system—which, from what she could tell, mainly consisted of the coastal road and a series of one-lane streets, switchbacks, and dirt paths that her sedan would probably conk out on—fell silent as she watched the couple's progress. Robyn glanced her way and was surprised to see that her expression looked haunted, her gaze faraway as she looked at the couple without appearing to actually see them.

"You okay?" she asked, peering at Helen in concern. By now, the couple had crossed onto the sand and were shedding their shoes as they headed for the shoreline.

"What's that?" Helen's gaze lingered on them for another few seconds before she gave a little start. "Sorry." She gave Robyn a sheepish smile. "I got lost in my own thoughts there for a hot second. Were you saying something?"

Robyn hesitated. She cast one last look at the couple before turning back to Helen, noting the shadow of sadness still lingering in her eyes. "No," she said finally. "I wasn't saying anything."

The next few minutes of the drive passed in silence, Robyn every so often glancing Helen's way to find the older woman staring out the window toward the distant mountains, one finger absentmindedly caressing a thick silver ring on her right hand. It was slightly tarnished from age but looked as though it had recently been polished, and the oval sapphire stone in the middle was shining. Some sort of insignia was carved into the band on either side of the stone, but Robyn couldn't read what it said.

"Class ring?" she asked, nodding to Helen's hand.

The older woman gave another start and blinked slowly at Robyn. "Sorry?"

Robyn gave her a gentle smile. "I was just admiring your ring. It looks similar to the one my parents bought me when I was a senior in high school."

"Oh. Yes." Helen stretched out her hand, and the sapphire caught the light. "This belonged to an old friend." Before Robyn could inquire further about the ring, and its owner, Helen pointed out the driver's side window and said, "Here we go—lifeguard tower number three. Just pull into that lot here and we'll get everything unloaded."

Robyn followed her directions, and a few moments later they were parked beside the sand, unloading grocery bags and containers of prepared foods. "Oh, good." Helen used one hand to shield her eyes from the sun's glare and the other to wave at a man halfway across the beach setting up a long folding table. "Owen's here already. Owen, yoo-hoo!" she called, cupping her hands around her mouth so her voice carried over the wind whipping off the ocean. "I'm a decrepit old woman and I need your help."

At the sight of Robyn's raised eyebrows, she shrugged and said, "What? If you're going to make it all the way to ninety-eight, it's only right that you enjoy some of the perks that come with it."

By now, the man was crossing the sand toward them, and as he got closer, Robyn saw that he was around the same age as her, with windswept blond hair threaded with gray, muscular arms and legs that spoke of plenty of time spent outdoors, and an easy, welcoming smile. "Hey there." He bent down to kiss Helen on the cheek, then straightened and held out his hand to Robyn. "First time I'm seeing you around. Welcome aboard—we could use all the help we can get."

"I'm happy to help," Robyn said, half-turning

from him to see another car pull into the parking lot. "But I'm afraid I don't actually know what I'm helping *with*. Helen hasn't been forthcoming about the details." The driver of the second car waved to the group, then popped his trunk and began unloading containers of food and groceries. "Is it some kind of… potluck?"

"In a manner of speaking," Owen said, motioning for Robyn to join him as he linked his arm through Helen's and began walking slowly across the sand with her. She grabbed as much food as she could and followed after him, her feet sinking further into the feather-soft sand with each step. When they finally reached the table, she was practically winded, and was grateful to set down some of the bags.

"Thistle Island is a great place to live," Owen said as he grabbed a second table from the sand and began unfolding its legs, "and the people here are hardworking, but like any other place in the world, some of them fall on hard times. Every week, those on the island who are able to do so contribute to our little community food bank, if you will, with fresh groceries and prepared dishes. We set everything up on the tables and in coolers, leave, and then whoever needs a helping hand stops by to grab what they need—no questions asked. Then one of our volunteers comes back in a couple of hours to pack up what's left."

Robyn glanced up at the seagulls already beginning to circle overhead. "Won't they get to it first?" she asked him, pointing at a particularly plump bird that landed a short distance away and watched them with beady orange eyes.

"They wish." Owen laughed, then jabbed his thumb over his shoulder at a pickup truck that had just arrived. "Lenny sets up the poles and bird netting every week—if you ever have a seagull problem in your garden, he's the man to call."

"I'll keep that in mind," Robyn said, unable to keep the smile from her lips. A few short days ago, having such a thing as a "seagull problem" at her house would have been unthinkable.

And completely ridiculous.

But here, apparently, it was just your average, run-of-the-mill problem. Robyn couldn't have been more charmed.

Ten minutes later, a small crowd was assembled on the sand, everyone working together seamlessly to get the food bank up and running. Introductions were made all around, and even though Robyn usually felt uncomfortable making small talk with strangers, they were a friendly, welcoming bunch who asked her questions about herself and seemed genuinely interested in hearing her answers. Her gaze drifted to Owen on more than a few occasions—he seemed to be the leader of the group, and she found herself admiring his efficiency, friendly attitude, and generous spirit.

"What's his story?" she asked Helen a little while later after they said their goodbyes and began their slow trek back across the sand toward the car. "Owen's, that is."

"We aren't too well-acquainted on a personal level," Helen said, gripping Robyn's arm as they navigated the sand. "But he's a lovely man—a teacher at the local high school and a big history buff. Don't get him started on something that happened three hundred years ago or you'll never get away. I made the mistake once of asking him a question about the French Revolution, and would you believe that I started out the conversation as a brunette and ended it with hair grayer than a witch's? Almost gave myself a heart attack when I got home and looked in the mirror. Why?" She shot Robyn a sly look. "Are you interested in him?"

"Oh, no." Robyn shook her head as Keith's face flashed through her mind. "Trust me, I'm not looking right now. Just trying to get to know my neighbors, I guess."

"Too bad." They reached the car, and Helen lowered herself into the passenger seat. "He's as solid as they come. Hard to imagine why he's single, but I've never asked him. I figure if he ever wanted to talk about his personal life with me, he would. People are entitled to their secrets." She absentmindedly rubbed the class ring again, and then, noticing Robyn's gaze tracking her movements, she covered it with one hand—whether purposely or not, Robyn couldn't tell.

"Well, let's get a move on," Helen said, buckling her seatbelt and waiting for Robyn to do the same. "All this sea air makes me hungry—or rather, I should say it makes my credit card hungry. I haven't had a proper shopping day in a long time, and besides, someone needs to be your official Thistle Island tour guide. Are you ready to hit the town?"

"You have no idea," Robyn said as she took a moment to inhale the fresh sea air before cranking the car to life and reaching for the radio. A few minutes later they were cruising down the coastal road once more, windows rolled down, belting out oldies songs at the top of their lungs, much to the amusement of the people they passed along the way.

Robyn didn't care if her singing voice was awful enough to send the seagulls scrambling for deeper waters. In that moment, she couldn't ever remember feeling more carefree.

∽

LATER THAT EVENING, after preparing dinner for Helen and wishing her a good night, Robyn struggled into her bungalow, both arms weighed down by shopping bags. The day had been a productive—and exhausting—one, with Helen dragging her from shop to shop, introducing her to the business owners and customers she knew. Robyn had never met so many people at once, and by the time lunch rolled around, she'd already forgotten the names of half of them.

She and Helen had enjoyed sandwiches and raspberry lemonades at a small café that overlooked the water, where they could watch the ships sailing to shore and the beachgoers splashing in the waves and building sand castles. The town itself was lovely; no cars were allowed in the main square, and so Robyn had parked on the outskirts and she and Helen had strolled along the cobblestone paths that wound around the shops and businesses, which were all

THE HARBOR HOUSE

painted in bright, cheerful colors and hung with equally bright awnings that fluttered softly in the ocean breeze. Plenty of outdoor seating was available for those who wished to admire the island's sweeping views, with benches and picnic tables set up at regular intervals beneath shady trees. The ocean was a shade of deep cerulean today, and the crystalline sky was dotted with wispy clouds that stretched out over the water.

They had taken their time exploring the shops, and Robyn had picked up a few things that she needed to make her new bungalow feel like home, including a beautiful set of soft blue curtains and a matching bedspread, an opalescent pink vase that would be perfect for holding seashells, and a painting of the island that had been created by a local artist, which she planned to hang in the small eating alcove off her kitchen.

By midday, Helen had started to flag, and even though she offered a few weak protests when Robyn suggested that they return home to rest, she had finally relented. She'd spent the remainder of the afternoon dozing in the Adirondack chair on her front porch, paperback book open in her lap, while Robyn performed a few light chores around the house and prepared dinner. After eating together on the back patio, where a spectacular sunset painted the sky in shades of coral and purple that Robyn didn't even know existed, they'd said their goodnights and gone their separate ways.

Deciding that she was too wiped to do much more than run a washcloth over her face and brush her teeth, Robyn sank beneath the covers with a book in her hand and a smile on her lips. It had been a good day, she decided as she felt herself drifting off to sleep.

And she couldn't wait to find out what tomorrow would bring.

CHAPTER 7

Robyn had just finished dressing the next morning when she heard a knock at the door and opened it to find Levi on the other side, his hands shoved in his pockets, his expression one of deep discomfort, as if speaking to her was the last thing on earth he wanted to be doing right now.

"Just wanted to check in and make sure you were getting along okay," he said by way of greeting. "Is there anything I can do for you? I know that bathroom sink can get a little leaky, so I have some tools in my truck if you'd like me to take a look at it before I head out for the morning."

"No, everything's been perfect," Robyn said, leaning against the doorframe, arms crossed over her chest. Then she hesitated. "I guess I heard the toilet running a few times overnight, but it wasn't anything serious. If you don't have time to—"

"I'll be right back." Levi turned abruptly and strode back to the main house, presumably to find his tools. He was wearing dirt-streaked jeans again, along with work boots and a white T-shirt that showcased his lean frame. Robyn found herself admiring him as he walked away, then laughed to herself and shook her head. Definitely *not* the type of man for her. She preferred spending time with people who actually said hello and goodbye, who had *manners*, for crying out loud.

Still, she knew from what Helen had told her that Levi was a good man—and she could see for herself how he went out of his way to take care of his great-aunt, to look after her and see that she had everything she needed. Robyn had yet to meet Delaney, his little girl, but she had seen her following her father around the backyard the evening she'd arrived on the island, holding a child's-size watering can to tend to the garden while he operated the hose. Robyn couldn't hear what they were saying, but she could see that the girl was chattering incessantly, and every time Levi turned his gaze on her, his face was softened into a smile.

Robyn's heart had ached as she watched them, mainly because she knew this little girl and her father had suffered a tremendous loss, one they would carry with them forever. But her heart had ached for another reason, too—Robyn had always believed that one day she would be a mother, but it seemed that life had other plans. She and Keith had talked about it on many occasions, and while he wasn't entirely opposed to the idea, he hadn't seemed excited about the prospect of fatherhood. So it became one more hope she put off, one more wish tucked away in the corner of her heart, one more thing about him she thought she could change.

And, at the end, one more reason to walk away.

Before she had time to reflect on this further, Levi was back, rounding the corner of his house with toolbox in hand. With a nod to Robyn, he stepped past her into the bungalow and made his way to the small bathroom next door to her bedroom. Debating whether or not to follow him— and then deciding that he definitely wouldn't prefer her company—Robyn headed for the kitchen instead to brew a pot of coffee and eat a quick bowl of cereal. Levi had been kind enough to stock her house with the essentials before she'd arrived, another point for him in the "nice" department, she decided as she sat down at the table.

She ate while listening to the sounds of Levi tinkering in the other room, every so often grunting or muttering something under his breath, and when she heard the clank of his toolbox shutting, she poured him a mug of coffee and headed down the hallway to meet him. She found him not in the bathroom, however, but standing frozen in the doorway of her bedroom, one hand gripping the doorframe, the other white-knuckling the handle of his toolbox as he stared inside the room.

"Can I help you with something?" she asked, annoyed at the invasion of privacy. If he needed something in there, he could have simply *asked* her. Of course, that would have required actual conversation, something he seemed to avoid at all costs.

One point toward the "rude and aloof" category.

He turned to her, and she was taken aback that his eyes were cold, his expression one of barely restrained anger. "Where are they?" he said, clenching his jaw. "You had no right to take them down."

"I—sorry?" Robyn stared at him in bewilderment. "I have no idea what you're talking about. I didn't take anything…"

And then her voice trailed off when she realized he was no longer looking at her; instead, his gaze was darting between the new curtains and bedspread she'd purchased just yesterday. "Oh, *that*?" She stepped aside him into the room, setting the mug of coffee down on the dresser and heading for the closet. "I have them right here," she said, opening the door and crouching down to retrieve them from the floor. She held the bundle out to him. "I wasn't going to throw them away. I just wanted something a little more... me." When his expression didn't change, she added, "They had some holes in them, too, so I figured—"

"You. Had. No. *Right*." The last word was practically a hiss as he stepped forward and grabbed the bundle from her arms. He shook them out, his eyes roving over them to make sure they were okay, and when he turned back to her, his cheeks were red and his jaw set. "These do not belong to you. They—"

"Daddy?"

They both jumped at the sound of the little girl's voice, and Robyn turned to find Delaney standing in the hallway behind them, eyes wide with alarm as she stared from her father to Robyn and back again. "What's going on?"

"Nothing." Levi recovered himself quickly,

crouching beside his daughter and studying her face intently. "What are you doing here?"

"I wanted to meet…" Delaney glanced up at Robyn uncertainly.

"Hi there," she started to say, shaking off her disbelief at the conversation that had just ensued and moving toward the little girl. "You must be—"

"We're going." Levi turned his daughter around and steered her toward the front door. Once she reached it, she glanced back over her shoulder at Robyn, then watched as her father gathered up the bedspread and curtains in his arms and strode toward her. A moment later they were gone, leaving Robyn to sag against the wall in shock as she watched them cross the yard and disappear into their own house.

What had just *happened*?

She was still staring out the window a few minutes later when Helen rounded the corner from her yellow cottage, her white hair wild, her turquoise glasses glinting in the early-morning sunshine. "I see you're an early riser like me," she said when she opened the door, brushing sand from her shoes before she stepped inside. "Like they say, the early bird catches the worm—or in my case, the early bird catches all the cream-filled donuts at the bakery. I have a dozen of the best little beauties you've ever tasted waiting on my back patio—are you interested? Levi and Delaney will be joining us too—I figure it's a good chance for all of us to get to know one another, seeing as we're stuck together now."

"No thanks," Robyn said quickly, ignoring the rumble in her stomach at the mention of the treats. "I was actually planning to go for a quick walk on the beach before I came over this morning. That is, if that's okay…?"

She held her breath while waiting for Helen to respond. The last thing, the absolute *last thing*, she needed right now was to sit across the table and make nice with the man who had just yelled at her—no, *raged* at her—over an old, slightly moldy bedspread, of all things. "Can I take you up on the offer another time?" she added, smiling sweetly at the older woman.

As in never. Never *ever*.

"Of course you can, especially since that means more for me." Helen gave her a wicked grin, then turned and headed back out the door. "If you change your mind, it'll be too late!" she called over her shoulder as she walked across the grass, the ocean breeze rippling the back of her shirt.

Robyn heaved a long, loud sigh as she watched her walk away, and then turned back into the house to search for her shoes. She hadn't been intending to go to the beach at all, but she hadn't been able to think up a better excuse for avoiding breakfast on the spot. Grabbing a thermos from the kitchen cabinet, she filled it up to the top with coffee, then slid on a light jacket and was out the door within minutes, ducking her head as she hurried past Levi's house to avoid an uncomfortable encounter.

Despite her confusion, embarrassment, and anger over what had just happened, Robyn found herself relaxing the moment her feet sank into the sand. She quickly unlaced her shoes, leaving them by the lifeguard tower and heading down to the shore, a sigh of contentment escaping her lips as the water lapped over her toes. She stood there for a long time, watching the ships bobbing along the horizon as the saltwater breeze blew strands of hair around her face and into her mouth, but she didn't bother brushing them away.

A short distance away, a seagull dipped in and out of the waves, no doubt searching for its breakfast, and farther out in the deep blue water, Robyn thought she caught the flash of a gray fin whipping out of the water, blink and you could miss it. The mountains rose up behind her, with colorful cottages and bungalows tucked here and there among the pine trees, and far to her left, a boardwalk stretched out into the sea.

The beach was mostly empty at this time of day, although as Robyn turned to begin her walk along the shore, she caught sight of a father and his young son heading toward the boardwalk, dented metal pails in hand, fishing lines slung over their shoulders. Beyond them, a young woman in a bodysuit was paddling into the water, surfboard at her side, sun highlighting the hints of gold in her hair.

The morning still held a chill in the air, and Robyn wrapped her arms around herself as she strolled along the waterline, stopping every so often when she caught the glint of a seashell poking up from the sand. A lone sand crab, its body an iridescent white, scuttled past her toes before burrowing into the sea-soaked sand, legs wriggling before disappearing beneath the waves. Somewhere overhead, a group of seagulls squawked to each other, their cries almost drowned out by the water crashing to shore.

Robyn didn't know how long she walked; she lost

track of time as she allowed herself to be swept away in the beauty surrounding her. As the sun rose higher in the sky, its rays dappling the water and warming her skin, she turned back, realizing that Helen's cheerful yellow house was now a pinprick in the distance. She started toward it, then stopped as she saw something glittering in the water not far from shore.

Using one hand to shield her eyes from the sun's glare, she took one step into the ocean and then another, squinting to try and make out the object dipping in and out of sight amid the churning water. On her third step, she saw it more clearly, and her heart skipped a beat in excitement as she realized what it was.

A glass bottle, still sealed with a cork, a tightly rolled piece of paper clearly visible inside.

Robyn shed her jacket and splashed out further to retrieve it, paddling against the waves, sprays of salty water landing on her tongue, in her eyes, soaking into her hair as she tried and failed to grasp it three times before finally succeeding. Tucking the bottle close to her side, she waded back to shore, shivering as she emerged onto the sand and doing her best to wring the water out of her now-soaked shirt and pants. She walked further up the beach and set the bottle gently in the sand before lowering herself down beside it. She turned it over, watching as the paper rolled with the movement of the bottle, and then examined the cork before thumbing it out with a *pop*.

Heart racing, she dried her hands as best she could, then untied the piece of blue ribbon wrapped around the paper. She unrolled it and spread it out on the sand, tucking her hair behind her shoulders to avoid dripping water onto the writing, which was elegant and neat, the ink slightly faded with time.

December 21, 2002

Dearest John,

Another Christmas is approaching. Another year is drawing to a close. And still I dream of your face each night. I hear your voice, your laughter, your whisper against my ear, and it is so easy for me to believe that you are with me. That I am whole once more.

Do you remember the night the snow fell on the estate? We waited until the rest of the world was asleep before sneaking outside, beneath the sky so dark it was practically black, and holding each other as the snowflakes swirled around us. I can still remember the silence, so thick, so welcoming after the months of fear and near misses. In that moment, the world was whole, and perfect. In that moment, we were whole. We were perfect.

And then Sir Corbyn found us wandering his grounds! I admit, I was sore with him at first for ruining that beautiful night, but when he invited us into his house and we enjoyed a glass of brandy by the fire, I almost, for just a moment, believed that life was normal. That it would be a Christmas for celebration, and family, and togetherness—and most of all, for love.

So many Christmases have passed without you. But still, I remember that night as clearly as though it were yesterday.

My darling, the sky is growing darker just like it did on that long-ago night, and it is time for me to go to bed. Please know that I will be thinking of you, as I always do, and forever will. Please know that the echo of your laughter is the only thing that brings me true comfort, if only in my dreams.

Forever Yours,

Rosie

When Robyn was finished reading, she sat back, fingers trembling against the page, and blinked furiously against the tears forming in her eyes. The beauty of the message, the heartbreak and the hope, the memories and the longing, nearly took her breath away. She turned the paper over, hoping to find an address, a full name, anything that would identify who Rosie was.

THE HARBOR HOUSE

But it was blank.

Robyn read the message a second time and then a third before carefully rolling up the paper and tucking it back inside the bottle for safekeeping. So engrossed was she in thoughts of what she had just read that she barely registered the walk back to Helen's house; before she realized it, she had reached the harbor, and quickly walked up the steps to the weathered dock, dodging people preparing to launch their boats into the water and seagulls swooping low over their heads, hoping to snag a treat.

She crossed the road to Helen's house, and was just about to knock on her front door when she heard voices drifting toward her from the back patio —and among them, notably, was Levi's.

And right now, he was the last person she wanted to share the message with.

Instead, she veered away from the door, glancing back over her shoulder once she reached the road to make sure that no one had spotted her. But Helen, Levi, and Delaney were still enjoying their breakfast, their chairs turned toward the mountains, allowing Robyn to slip away unnoticed. With nowhere to go, and the bottle still clutched firmly in one hand, she decided to find someplace to pass the time until Levi presumably—hopefully—left for work and she could show Helen what she had found.

She headed in the opposite direction, walking along the pedestrian path that paralleled the coastal road until she came to the path that led toward the island's main square, already bustling with tourists and residents alike. Robyn wandered along the cobblestone walkways for a few minutes before the aroma of coffee and pastries drifted toward her on the ocean breeze, causing her stomach to growl and reminding her that in the excitement of the morning, she hadn't eaten much in the way of breakfast.

Following her nose, she passed a bookshop and women's clothing boutique before arriving at a small coffee shop beneath a bright pink awning with white lettering that spelled out The Coral Café. A few tables were set up outside beneath yellow and pink umbrellas, each occupied by couples or solo diners enjoying their morning coffee while watching the ships sailing out from the harbor below, their white masts sparkling against the indigo sea.

The interior was cozy and inviting, with a small seating area on the left and a library of sorts on the right, complete with dark brown leather chairs and couches and a gray stone fireplace lined with flickering candles. Floor-to-ceiling shelves crammed with books flanked the fireplace alongside a handwritten sign that said *Give a book, take a book*, and the picture windows that lined the front of the coffee shop offered breathtaking views of the island and the ocean beyond.

Robyn stepped into line behind a young couple with beach bags and flipflops, eyes scanning the chalkboard menu behind the counter. "Can I help you?" a pretty woman about her own age asked when it was her turn at the register. Robyn ordered a hazelnut latte and croissant, paid, and stepped aside, and as she did so, the woman caught sight of the bottle tucked under her arm. "Found another one?" she asked, raising her eyebrows and nodding toward it with a knowing smile.

"Another... what?" Robyn frowned at her, then at the bottle. "There's more than one?"

The woman laughed. "You must be new to Thistle Island." She opened her mouth to say more, but then the bell above the shop's door chimed and an elderly man stepped inside and made his way up to the counter. "Tell you what," she said to Robyn, handing her the latte and croissant and nodding toward the chairs arranged in front of the fireplace. "Give me ten minutes until my assistant comes back from break and I'll give you the scoop on our island's greatest mystery."

Intrigued, Robyn thanked the woman and headed for the chairs, selecting one near the window with a view of the island's lighthouse in the distance. She set the bottle gently on the table in front of her, then spent the next few minutes sipping her latte and perusing the titles on the bookshelves, every so often glancing toward the counter, where the woman was busy helping the customers continually streaming through the door. The coffee shop seemed to be popular, and for good reason, Robyn decided as she bit into the buttery croissant that practically melted on her tongue.

After what seemed like an eternity, given Robyn's mounting interest in what the woman had to say about the mysterious message that had washed ashore, a teenage girl appeared from the back of the shop, wrapped an apron around her waist, and took her place behind the counter. The woman said something to the girl, nodded in Robyn's direction, and then untied her own apron before heading for the chair beside Robyn.

"Whew, I'm beat," she said, brushing a few strands of auburn hair back from her face and sinking into the leather chair. "You'd think after more than a decade in business I'd get used to the summer rush, but every year once June rolls around I'm taken by surprise. I guess I get complacent during the colder months." She smiled and held out her hand to Robyn. "I'm Brooke. I own The Coral Café. I haven't seen you around before—tourist or newcomer?"

"A little of both, I guess," Robyn said, smiling back at her. "I recently started a part-time job here as a companion to a woman named Helen Moore, and I moved into her nephew's guest house."

"Ah, Helen. She's one of my favorite people on the planet." Brooke shook her head, grinning. "She might be small, but she's mighty. Every time I see her, I tell her that I want to be her when I grow up." Then she cocked her head, studying Robyn's face. "You're living in Levi's guest house, huh? Tell me, has the man said two words to you since you moved in?"

"More or less." Robyn shifted uncomfortably in her chair, feeling her cheeks redden as she tried once more to forget their encounter that morning. "Delaney seems like a sweetheart, though," she said, trying to change the subject.

"She is," Brooke acknowledged. "Sara was a good friend of mine—we all grew up on the island together. Her death was shocking, and awful, and... I don't even have words for it." She sighed heavily. "But she'd be proud of the way Levi's been raising their daughter. It can't be easy doing it all on his own." The two women fell silent for a moment before Brooke nodded toward the bottle. "So you've found the latest installment in the saga of Rosie and John."

"Apparently so." Robyn leaned forward in her chair eagerly. "I've never come across a message in a bottle before—and now you're telling me there's more than one? How is that even possible?"

"I have no idea." Brooke gestured toward the bottle. "May I?"

"Be my guest." Robyn popped the cork once more and shook out the tightly rolled piece of paper inside, watching as Brooke scanned it quickly. She had the same reaction that Robyn did to the beautiful love letter, and had to take a moment to dab at her eyes with the sleeve of her shirt before passing the message back to Robyn, who secured it inside the bottle once more.

"Just as heartbreaking as the others," Brooke said, clearing her throat and giving Robyn a watery smile. "We've found five other letters—the first one way back in the 1970s, I think, and the most recent before this one was... oh, probably about six or seven years ago. Always from Rosie to her dearest John, always filled with the most beautiful memories. The rest of them are stored at the Thistle Island Historical Society." Then she laughed. "Which sounds pretty impressive, but it's really a one-room collection of the island's history that a friend of mine named Owen has compiled. It's displayed at the local library."

"I've met Owen." Robyn perked up at the mention of his name. "He runs the food bank on the beach."

"The very same." Brooke nodded. "Anyway, he has the rest of the letters in his collection. You can stop by the library anytime during business hours and read them." She sighed. "But unfortunately, they won't tell you much. No one knows who Rosie is, or John, or where they lived, or when they were together, or what happened to them. Once every decade or so, one of these messages washes up somewhere on the island's beaches. Me and everyone else I know obsesses about them for a while, and then we forget about it until another one washes to shore. It's become our little mystery, but we're no closer to solving it than we were fifty years ago."

Brooke glanced at the clock on the wall. "Tell you

what. I'm planning to leave Dani in charge of the shop for the rest of the day, so if you give me a few minutes to wrap things up, I'd be happy to take you there. It's been a while since I've read the letters, and besides, I have to tell Owen that I've set up a date for him on Friday night."

"A date?" Robyn raised her eyebrows. "Are the two of you—"

"No, no," Brooke interrupted with a laugh. "Friends only. But over the past few years, I've managed to successfully set up a few of the island's residents, and somewhere along the way I developed a reputation as the unofficial Thistle Island matchmaker. Owen's been my biggest challenge—probably because he keeps insisting he doesn't want to be set up. But I know he's lonely, and he's a good catch, so I'm trying to find him 'the one.'" She made air quotes with her fingers. "I figure if I go down to the library and catch him off guard, he'll agree to meet Tabitha." She stood from the chair and glanced toward the front of the shop, where the line was beginning to die down.

"Meet you out front in five minutes?" she asked. "Then we can head over to the library together."

"Definitely." Robyn stood too. As Brooke walked

away, she polished off the rest of her croissant, then grabbed the bottle and headed for the exit.

An argument with her new landlord, a message in a bottle, and maybe, just maybe, a new friend—it wasn't even noon yet, and this day was promising to be Robyn's most exciting one on Thistle Island yet.

CHAPTER 8

After making a quick call to Helen's house to make sure she didn't need anything—and audibly sighing with relief when Levi didn't answer the phone—Robyn waited for Brooke to emerge from the coffee shop and together they set off toward the library.

"How do you know Owen's going to be there?" Robyn asked as they headed away from the island's main square toward a treelined path that overlooked the shimmering water. Both sides of the path were lined with plants blooming with colorful flowers and tall grass that brushed against their legs as they walked.

"Because he's always there," Brooke said, stepping aside so a young family carrying beach towels and folding chairs could pass by them. "When he's not teaching, he's holed up at the library, reading through as many books as he can. It's been that way ever since…" Her voice trailed off as she seemed to reconsider what she was saying. "Well, for a long time."

Robyn eyed her, but asked no further questions. The last thing she wanted to do was come off as a busybody—in a community as small as Thistle Island, that would likely earn her a reputation that wouldn't endear her to anyone. She and Brooke chatted as they walked, and Robyn learned that the willowy redhead with the striking green eyes had been born and raised on the island, leaving only for a few years to earn a college degree in business and marketing and then returning to learn the ropes in various cafés and restaurants before opening up The Coral Café ten years ago. She seemed to know everyone and everything about Thistle Island, and regaled Robyn with stories of several residents she had yet to meet.

"So… Levi," Robyn said tentatively, unsure why she was bringing up Helen's nephew but feeling compelled to learned more about him. "He seems a little… angry."

Brooke sighed and shook her head sadly. "He is,

and in all fairness, he has every right to be. He and Sara were childhood sweethearts—you never saw one without the other. They were married right out of high school. I was one of her bridesmaids, and it was a beautiful day, filled with the kind of love and joy every girl dreams about for her wedding. The look in Levi's eyes when she walked down the aisle toward him..." Brooke's voice caught, and she cleared her throat. "Well, I'll never forget it."

A heaviness settled over Robyn's chest as Brooke spoke, though whether out of sadness for Levi and Sara, or the loss of her own dreams of marriage and happily ever after, she couldn't say. "So what happened to her?" she asked, wondering if she had been too quick to judge Levi for his unapproachable nature. "Sara, I mean."

"She died the day after Delaney was born," Brooke said softly, a faraway look in her eyes as she stopped walking and gazed out over the water far below them. Robyn joined her, and together they watched a young couple on the beach who were dipping their baby's toes in and out of the waves, laughing as she squealed with delight. "It was all so sudden—one minute she was there, and the next minute she was gone. I had just gone to see her a few hours before... before it happened."

Her voice cracked again. "She had a pulmonary embolism, and in the blink of an eye, Levi lost the love of his life and became a single father to a newborn. A lot of men would have cracked under the grief and the pressure, but Levi did everything he could to make sure that little girl has grown up in a loving home. He was always the strong and silent type, but ever since Sara died, he's mostly cut himself off from everyone on the island, except for his daughter and his great-aunt. He spends the majority of his time outdoors, on his own, taking care of things around the island. He's the ranger, and all of this"—she swept her arm around to encompass the beauty surrounding them—"is his responsibility, and it's not one he takes lightly."

"Wow," Robyn murmured, her eyes following Brooke's hand. "I had no idea."

They lapsed into silence after that, following the path a short distance until they reached the Thistle Island library, a surprisingly large one-level building made of green stucco trimmed in white. There were plenty of tall windows thrown open to let in the fresh sea air, and the library was surrounded by majestic dogwood trees that provided plenty of shade to the benches lining the sidewalk that circled the building.

Brooke led the way to the front door, waving a friendly hello to the librarian behind the front desk before bypassing the rows of shelves and comfortable-looking couches and recliners where patrons were reading books, magazines, and newspapers. In the very back of the library, past the children's section, which featured a stunning hand-painted mural of jungle animals on parade, a narrow door led to a small room with a few display cases and tables. There, in the corner of the room, sitting on a folding metal chair and completely engrossed in a thick book with a broken spine and yellowing pages, was Owen.

He glanced up at the sound of their footsteps, blinking at Brooke slowly in surprise before his eyes landed on Robyn and he gave her a genuine smile. "Well hello there," he said, carefully bookmarking his page before standing to greet her with a handshake. "I see you've found my little corner of the library. Are you here to learn more about Thistle Island? I've made it my mission to collect whatever pieces of our history I can find and display them here."

Then he noticed the bottle tucked securely under Robyn's arm, and his eyes lit up. "You found another one!"

"That's why we're here," Brooke said, stepping

forward to greet Owen with a quick kiss on the cheek. "The latest message just washed up on the beach this morning. I told Robyn about the others we've found over the years, and she wanted to stop in and take a look at them."

"Absolutely." Owen gestured for Robyn to follow him to a small glass case in one corner of the room. As they approached it, she could see that it contained the other five letters, each carefully laminated and labeled and displayed beneath its corresponding bottle. She read and reread each letter, searching for clues as to the mystery writer and her beau, but by the end, her eyes were clouded with tears and she was no closer to learning anything more about Rosie and John than she had been on the beach that morning.

"They're beautiful, aren't they?" Owen said from beside her, leaning over and pressing his fingertips gently against the case. "Each letter makes me feel like I'm right there with Rosie and John, witnessing their love story. These messages have almost become island lore—no one knows where they come from, how they got here, if any more will wash up. The first few we found used to be housed in the mayor's office, but when I set out to start my collection here at the library, I approached him and asked for his permission to relocate them. He readily agreed that they should be part of it—maybe one of the most important parts."

He held out his hand for the bottle Robyn was holding. "May I?"

"Of course." She uncorked it, shook out the letter, and passed it to him. While he read it, lips moving silently as his eyes scanned the page, she bent low over the display case to once again read the first letter that had washed to shore.

May 8, 1965

Dearest John,

Twenty years ago today, the world celebrated. I can still remember the soldiers dancing in the streets. One of them grabbed me and twirled me around, both of us laughing and crying, neither one of us believing that the end had finally come. He looked nothing like you, but in his eyes, I saw only yours. That day, I was so filled with hope, and happiness, and the belief that the future was bright with possibilities.

And it has been, in many ways. But in the only way that truly matters, it has not.

I miss you.

Tonight, I celebrate alone. But I am never truly alone, am I? For I know, when I look to the heavens, that you are always with me.

All my love, now and forever,
Rosie

"I can't believe it," Owen muttered from somewhere behind her. Robyn turned, pulling herself away from the letter to find his face lit up with excitement that bordered on ecstasy. "We finally have a clue—an actual, solid clue."

He jogged over to the display case, tapping the glass directly above the letter she had just finished reading. "Up until now, we only knew that Rosie and John were together sometime before or during World War II." He jabbed his finger at the date written on the first letter. "May 8, 1965 is twenty years after V-E Day, which was when Germany surrendered and the war in Europe came to an end. Even though it wasn't the official end of the war, it was a day of celebration in the United States and all throughout the world."

He laughed and raked his fingers through his blond hair while shaking his head in disbelief. "But trying to find a soldier named John is like sifting through the world's biggest haystack. Where to even begin? More than seventy million people served in the armed forces at that time, and John isn't exactly an uncommon name. We've suspected from the start that John and Rosie's story somehow revolves around the most devastating war the world has ever seen, but that's as far as we got. But *this* letter"—he waved it excitedly in Robyn's face—"might have just changed everything."

"How?" she asked, feeling her own excitement mounting. Given the turmoil she'd been experiencing in her personal life recently, getting swept away in Rosie and John's love story had provided a much-needed respite from her own pain. It had erased Keith's face, and her father's, and replaced them with an image of a young couple holding each other under the stars as the snowflakes glittered in the night air around them. It had allowed her to imagine, for just a few moments, that she was as loved as Rosie had been.

"This name right here." He pointed at the page. "Sir Corbyn, the man who found them outside and invited them in for a drink. I have no idea who he is or how he might be important to the story, but it's a starting point. An actual, tangible starting point." He rubbed his hands together gleefully. "I'm going to get started on my research right now." Smiling at Robyn, he added, "Would you like to help me?"

"I'd love to," she said, and then caught sight of her watch and hesitated. "But I'm due back at Helen's house in less than an hour, and I don't want to get wrapped up in something I can't finish." She gave Owen a pleading look. "You'll wait for me, won't you? Since I found the most important clue, I feel like you owe me that much," she added with a wink.

"You drive a hard bargain," he said, gazing down at the letter forlornly. "But I guess I don't have much choice, do I?" He laughed. "Tell you what. Why don't the three of us meet at my house tonight, and we'll see what we can find."

Brooke shot Owen a dubious look. "And you promise you won't start without us? I have a hard time believing you're going to spend the next six hours doing anything but Googling furiously."

He frowned at her. "I have willpower, you know."

Her eyebrows practically disappeared into her hairline. Robyn glanced back and forth between the two of them in amusement.

"Fine," he relented. "I'll cut you a deal—you bring the pizza, and I'll give you my word that I won't even *open* my laptop until you get there."

"*Or* your books. Or anything here at the library." She crossed her arms over her chest.

His smile dimmed and he pursed his lips, thinking hard. Finally he groaned and said, "You got me. And you've got yourself a deal." He held out his hand, and they shook. Then, as if to make a point, he passed Rosie's latest letter back to Robyn, then turned back to the book he had been reading when they arrived and buried his nose in it.

"You're dismissed," he added without glancing up.

"Come on," Brooke said with a grin, tugging Robyn toward the door. "Let's get out of here before he changes his mind."

A few moments later, they were outside in the sunshine, the birds singing in the trees around them as they headed back toward town. As she walked, Robyn had to restrain herself from joining them in song. She'd only moved to Thistle Island a few days ago, but she was already falling in love with the town—and the people.

With one very notable exception.

But even that, she decided as she turned her face up to the cloudless sky to soak in the sun's warmth, was still very much up for debate.

~

To Robyn's disappointment, Helen had taken the news about the message in a bottle with a shrug, wave of one hand, and a "Pah" without bothering to look up from the book she was reading on the front porch.

"I thought you'd be more excited," Robyn said, feeling slightly deflated as she gazed down at the bottle in her hand. "Owen couldn't wait to get his hands on it."

"I told you, Owen likes history, and from everything I've read in those letters, Rosie and John are old history." She glanced up from the book, turquoise glasses sparkling in the sunlight. "*If* they're even real. I'm still undecided over whether this whole 'mystery' isn't someone's idea of a practical joke."

"Who would do that?" Robyn frowned as she rolled the bottle in one hand, watching as the letter rolled along with it. Then she shook her head and said, "Uh-uh, sorry, I'm not buying that. Rosie's words are so, so... *real*, and the pictures she paints in her letters to John are as vivid as this." She waved her hand in a semi-circle to encompass the island scenery around them. "No one could write the things I've read in those letters without experiencing —and losing—true love."

Helen paused for a moment, gazing out at the gently rolling ocean before turning back to Robyn and raising one shoulder in a halfhearted shrug.

"Maybe you're right. But I've never quite understood the fixation on those letters. Even if they are real, whoever wrote them probably doesn't want to be identified, which is why they're thrown into the ocean in the first place. They're private, and I'm a firm believer that everyone's entitled to a little bit of privacy."

"You have a point." Robyn felt herself deflating further. Was she doing the right thing by trying to track down the real people behind the beautiful letters? If their love story began during the World War II era, chances were overwhelming that Rosie was no longer even alive. And if the heartache in those messages was as real as Robyn believed it to be, then John had been gone for much longer.

Helen studied Robyn's face for a moment, her gaze scrutinizing. "This is something you need to do, isn't it? For yourself, for whatever's going on in your life that you've been so reluctant to talk about."

Robyn swallowed hard, blinking back the tears forming rapidly at the corners of her eyes. Even though she'd only found the letter a few hours ago, the prospect of focusing on something that wasn't her own heartbreak, even for a moment or two, was nothing short of a gift. Since arriving on the island, she'd been in turmoil, constantly questioning whether the decisions she'd made about Keith, about her father, about her life and the things she wanted for herself and her future, were the right ones.

Had she become so fixated on the idea of marriage, of a solid commitment from the man who, by all accounts, had committed himself to her in his own way, that she'd given up her one chance at love? At happiness? At a future where she'd grow old with a solid, dependable, loving man by her side?

She had no way of knowing, and that alone was almost more than she could bear.

A lone tear tracked down her cheek and, embarrassed, Robyn hastened to wipe it away. "I guess I do need this," she said, tracing one finger down the bottle. "A distraction, a chance to put my time and energy into something else, just for a little while. The answers don't even matter all that much."

Helen rose from her chair and shuffled toward Robyn, placing a hand on her shoulder and giving her a soft smile. "Then why in the world are you listening to me? Go out there and find them. And when you do, be sure to tell me all about it. I could use some excitement in my life."

She gave Robyn's shoulder a gentle pat, then began shooing her toward the guest house next door. "Now why don't you take some time to yourself. I can't think of a better thing to do right now than take a nap, and I won't be able to get a single wink of sleep with you clattering around outside my bedroom door, fussing about like a mother hen."

Robyn opened her mouth to protest, knowing that Helen was only sending her away for her own benefit, but the older woman shook her head and gave her a severe look. "Now don't make me repeat myself," she scolded. "I only have so many words left in my life, and I intend to make each one of them count."

And with that, she gave Robyn a little push toward the grass, watching with arms crossed as she reluctantly made her way across the lawn toward her bungalow.

Once inside, Robyn brewed a mug of honey lavender tea and collapsed onto the living room couch, resting her head against the pillows and heaving a long sigh. Thoughts wandering toward Keith, and wondering what he was doing at this very second—was he missing her?—she slipped her hand into her pocket and withdrew her phone, tapping it idly against her thigh for several seconds before sliding open the screen and rereading the last message he had sent to her.

I miss you already. Please reconsider.

The words didn't have the same longing, the yearning, the passion that she was swept away in every time she read one of Rosie's letters to John, but Keith had never been a man of flowery words or overly grand gestures. He had loved her in a solid, quiet way, showing her how he felt every time he surprised her by cooking dinner after a long day of work, or letting her choose what movie they would watch on a Friday night, or fixing things around the house without her having to ask him. And she had done the same for him, always stocking up on his favorite foods during grocery store trips, making sure his work clothes were washed and hung in the closet, preparing homemade chicken soup when he was sick.

Ten years of the little things that, in the end, had all amounted to nothing.

Why hadn't she been enough?

A soft tapping at the front door interrupted her thoughts and, grateful for the distraction, Robyn slid her phone back into her pocket before padding over to the foyer to answer it. When she pulled it open, she was surprised to find not Helen, as she had been expecting, or even Levi, but a small girl with long black hair and beautiful hazel eyes.

"Delaney!" Robyn gave her a kind smile. "What

are you doing here?" She leaned out the door to search for Levi, but he was nowhere to be seen. She looked back at the girl, puzzled. "Is there something I can help you with?"

She stepped out onto the porch and gestured for the girl to take a seat in one of the matching Adirondack chairs. Delaney did so without hesitation, plopping into the one nearest her and swinging her legs as she studied Robyn with wide, interested eyes.

"Would you like some lemonade?" Robyn asked, her voice hesitant, as she took the seat beside her. Even though she had always adored children and wanted several of her own, she didn't have much experience with them—and, as a result, had no idea what to say to the seven-year-old girl watching her so intently. She was also keenly and uncomfortably aware that Delaney had witnessed the scene between her and Levi that morning.

"No thank you," the little girl said sweetly, then looked down at her hands, which were clasped in her lap. When she gazed up at Robyn again, her eyes were filled with uncertainty. "I'm not supposed to be here. Daddy said I shouldn't bother you."

"Oh, well, that's not necessary." Robyn frowned at her. "You're welcome to visit anytime, as long as your father is okay with it."

But Delaney didn't respond. Instead, she took a deep breath and said, "Don't be mad at him, okay? My daddy. For yelling at you this morning. He was just sad."

"He was sad?" Robyn echoed, studying the little girl's face. "Why was he sad?"

Delaney shrugged, now watching her hands once more. "He's always sad. He tries to hide it, but I can tell. But today, that bedspread he took away, and those curtains, they're special. My mom picked them out a long time ago, and they've always been in our guest house."

She raised her head and gave Robyn an imploring look. "She died a long time ago, and he misses her. He didn't mean to yell, and I know he's sorry."

Robyn felt her throat closing up, and she swallowed hard to keep her composure. "Well thank you for sharing that with me," she said, trying to cover up the crack in her voice. "I didn't know they belonged to your mother, and I'm sure they are very special. I'm not mad at your dad, and this helps me understand it better."

Delaney beamed at Robyn, her entire face lighting up. "Can I come visit sometime?"

"Of course you can." Robyn smiled back at her. "I would love for you to stop by. I've been meaning to tell you how much I love the stepping stones you painted." She waved her hand toward the path of stones leading from Levi's house to the guest cottage. "You're very talented."

The girl's smile grew, if possible, even wider. "Can we paint one together?"

By now, Robyn felt as though her heart would split in two from the adorableness. "We absolutely can. As long as your daddy says it's okay, why don't you come over tomorrow morning, and you can teach me how to do it." She grinned at her. "I *really* like your llama."

"Delaney!"

Both of them turned to find Levi striding across the lawn toward Robyn's house, his eyes on his daughter. "What are you doing here?" Folding his arms over his chest, he glanced from her to Robyn and back again. "You shouldn't be bothering Ms. Wright."

Robyn was on her feet in an instant, shaking her head. "Oh no, really, it's okay. We were just having a lovely—"

"Come on." Levi's voice was gentle but stern as he beckoned to his daughter with one finger.

She immediately jumped up from the chair, gave Robyn a regretful look, and then bounded down the porch steps to her father. Levi drew her toward him and then glanced back to Robyn. He opened his mouth as if he wanted to say something but then closed it again. With a gruff shake of his head, he muttered, "Sorry about that," and then turned and began steering Delaney across the lawn.

Robyn watched them go, and then suddenly called out, "Levi!"

He stopped and swung back toward her, head cocked slightly to one side, as she descended the porch steps and crossed the lawn toward them. She stopped a few feet away and gave him a tentative smile, Delaney's words ringing in her ears, then took a deep breath and said, "It's okay. Just... forget about it."

The meaning behind her words was clear, and Levi hesitated for a moment before giving her a brief nod and a tip of his hat. When he turned away once more, she caught sight of his face—

And could have sworn he was almost, *almost*, smiling.

CHAPTER 9

*L*ater that evening, Brooke swung by the harbor to pick up Robyn, and together they drove along the coastal road, enjoying the coral and purple sunset that spread its fingers out over the glittering water as they made their way to Owen's house, two large pizzas accompanying them in the car's backseat. Robyn watched the island scenery coast by, was dimly aware of Brooke singing along—badly—to an eighties pop song on the radio, but had a hard time concentrating on the exciting evening ahead.

Instead, her thoughts were filled with Delaney, and Levi, and everything she had heard that day.

He's always sad. He tries to hide it, but I can tell.

Robyn's heart settled somewhere in the pit of her

stomach as she recalled the little girl's words, saw once more the sorrow weighing heavily in her eyes, a feeling no child should ever have to endure. What must life have been like for her, growing up without a mother's guiding hand? And what must each day, week, month, *year*, have been like for Levi, trying to navigate the constantly twisting road of parenthood entirely on his own.

No wonder he was gruff. No wonder he was unreachable.

Had she misjudged him? Been unfair in her assessment?

Maybe he wasn't rude, or aloof, or any other unflattering words she could pick out of a thesaurus and throw at him. Maybe he was just deeply, deeply sad.

At times like these, it was impossible not to think of her own father, too. The loss of Robyn's mother had affected her father just as deeply. His sadness had been just as enduring, as all-consuming, as bottomless.

Now—and on the persistent advice of his daughters, no less—he was reaching out into the void, desperately grasping for a chance at happiness. According to him, at long last, he had found it.

And how had Robyn reacted to the news?

She couldn't have hurt him worse if she had slapped him in the face.

"You okay?"

Robyn blinked to find Brooke squinting at her in concern, one hand on the wheel, the other dangling out the window, fingers splayed, to enjoy the sea breeze. At the sight of Robyn's expression, which she hadn't been quick enough to hide, she fiddled with the radio dial, lowering the volume of the music to barely a whisper. "Need someone to talk to?"

She sighed heavily, leaning her head against the seat and staring out the car at the darkening sky. A chill had settled over the island, the wind blowing in off the ocean and swaying the bows of the pine trees that loomed over them, majestic, in the waning light. "I was just thinking of Levi."

Brooke shot her a knowing look. "Handsome, isn't he? I'm not surprised you're interested. In the first few years after Sara died, it seemed like every single woman within a hundred-mile radius was sniffing around, hoping for her chance to 'save' him. And when they found out he had a baby girl as well?" She let out a snort of disdain. "It was like dogs to a fire hydrant. They couldn't pee on him any faster if they tried."

"Wow." Robyn stared at her, half horrified, half

amused. "Thanks for that image. But no—I'm not interested in Levi. *Believe* me." She let out a snort of her own. "I was just thinking about how hard it must have been for him to lose his wife, and for Delaney to lose her mother. My mother died tragically too, and I still carry it with me to this day. My father was a wreck, but at least my sister and I were old enough to take care of ourselves. More or less," she added, thinking once more of Claire's impetuous behavior in the aftermath of the accident.

"Did he ever remarry?" Brooke asked, tapping the breaks to allow a seagull to safely waddle across the road. "I had always hoped that Levi would find someone eventually, even if it was just for Delaney's sake, but he's never been interested in putting himself out there."

"He's... engaged." The word sounded bitter on Robyn's tongue. At the sight of Brooke's raised eyebrows, she launched into an explanation of the disastrous pancake brunch, finishing with a description of Jessie that had her new friend nodding along knowingly.

"I would have freaked too," she said. "Have you spoken to him since?"

"No." The guilt in Robyn's tone was obvious. "Should I? I'm having a hard time envisioning how that conversation is going to go. I still don't approve of the relationship, and I can't pretend that I do."

Brooke shrugged. "Probably. I mean, he's your dad, right? At the end of the day, isn't family one of the most important things in life? Besides, you don't even know her—maybe they're good together. And if they're not, and it all comes crashing down around him, he's going to need your support."

Robyn laughed hollowly. "Now you sound like my sister."

Brooke grinned at her. "Then your sister sounds like a very wise woman."

By now, they had turned off the coastal road and onto a narrow, one-lane street bordered on both sides by magnificent dogwood trees. Behind them sat a row of neat bungalows, each painted a different pastel color and situated on lush lawns bursting with greenery and flowering bushes. Brooke parked at the curb in front of a small blue bungalow with a wrought-iron gate and a small vegetable garden. A chocolate Labrador was sniffing around the yard, bone dangling from his mouth, trying to find the perfect burying spot.

"Hey, Duke," Brooke said, reaching over the fence to stroke the dog's silky head as he came running over to greet them, bone now lying forgotten at his feet. He barked once at Robyn, then cocked his head, golden eyes assessing her as she stretched out her hand for him to sniff. He did so once, then licked it, tail wagging happily; she decided she must have passed the stranger-danger test with flying colors.

"You better not have forgotten the pizza," Owen called from the front door, leaning against the frame, muscular arms crossed over his chest as he smiled at them. He wore glasses pushed up onto his blond hair, giving him a professorial look, and a textbook was tucked under one arm.

"And *you* better not have started without us," Brooke said, nodding to the book as she gave Duke one last pat before reaching into the car's backseat for the pizzas. Robyn opened the gate, and the two of them met Owen at the door, Duke tagging along behind them, brown nose twitching as he sniffed hopefully at the pizza-saturated air.

"I kept my word, but I have to admit, it wasn't easy." Owen tossed Robyn an easy smile over his shoulder as he led them into the small living room. It was cozy but cluttered, with books and other reference materials stacked on every available surface, and what looked like an entire army's worth of papers waiting to be graded.

"Nothing better to do on a Saturday night than

read through a high school kid's best attempt at explaining the Cold War," he said with a laugh when he noticed Robyn glancing over the papers. "Luckily it's the final one of the year—and then, freedom." He stretched his arms behind his head and grinned widely; Robyn could have sworn she caught, out of the corner of her eye, Brooke shoot him a look of appreciation.

But it was gone in an instant. Instead, she turned to Robyn and said, "Don't let him fool you. He lives for grading papers and boring us all to tears with things that happened a thousand years ago that no one cares about anymore."

She nudged Owen aside and set the pizzas on what little available space there was on the coffee table. "Now go." She shooed him toward the kitchen with both hands. "You're in the company of women tonight. Plates and napkins are required so you can think we're dainty."

As soon as he was gone, she flipped open the lid of the topmost box and grabbed a slice of pizza dripping with melted cheese, then motioned for Robyn to do the same. Both slices were inhaled by the time Owen returned, balancing paper plates, a stack of napkins, and a six-pack of soda. He raised his eyebrows in amusement at the sight of the missing slices but made no comment, instead grabbing his laptop from the nearby desk and flipping it open.

"Join me," he said to Robyn, lowering himself onto the couch and patting the cushion beside him. "I've been thinking about Sir Corbyn all day, and I can't wait to dig in—something about the name rings familiar, but I can't quite put my finger on it." He pulled up the search window on his laptop and keyed in the name *Sir Corbyn*. "I'm guessing by the title and what vague details we have that Corbyn lived in England—which fits my World War II theory."

"And what is your World War II theory?" Robyn asked, leaning closer to view the screen, second slice of pizza already forgotten on her plate.

But Owen wasn't listening—he was eagerly scrolling through the search results, fingers moving rapid-fire on his trackpad, eyes scanning down the length of the page. Somewhere behind them, Brooke was working on her third slice, Duke at her feet, eyes wide as he silently begged.

"Don't give him any," Owen called over his shoulder just as Brooke was dangling a cheese glob Duke's way. "Unless you want to clean it up when it makes its grand reappearance all over the carpet."

She wrinkled her nose and snatched back the

cheese inches from Duke's open mouth, and the dog sat back on his haunches, whining in disappointment.

Owen was muttering to himself as he perused the search results, and then, upon reaching the middle of the second page, he snapped his fingers and said, "Here! Sir Edwin Corbyn. This looks promising."

He immediately clicked on the corresponding webpage, lips moving silently as he scrolled down the lines of text faster than Robyn could even begin to keep up. He stopped at a black-and-white picture of a gray-haired gentleman, maybe mid-sixties, with a round face and kind eyes, and jabbed his finger at the screen.

"He was a bigwig in the British automobile industry—he had a plant that manufactured car parts, one of the first in England. Look here!" His pitch rose in excitement as, behind him, Brooke moved closer to see over his shoulder. "During the Second World War, at the request of Prime Minister Winston Churchill, he halted all production related to automobiles and began building parts for the Royal Air Force instead. He and his team supplied parts for most of the British warplanes, and were instrumental in helping England fend off the Luftwaffe."

"What's the Luftwaffe?" Robyn asked, gently nudging Duke away with her knee when he turned doe eyes on her plate.

"Germany's air force." Owen leaned in closer to the screen, scrutinizing Sir Corbyn's photograph. "They were incredibly sophisticated—arguably the best air force in the world at the time—and they were relentless in their bombing attacks across Britain. They essentially terrorized the British population for years—no one knew when they would strike, or where. The damages and casualties were overwhelming."

"So what do you think this has to do with Rosie and John?" Brooke asked, her long auburn hair falling over Owen's shoulder as she leaned in closer to study the photograph. "Do you think they worked with him at his production plant?"

"No." Smiling, Owen shook his head. "This is where we'll see if my theory is correct. Anyone care to take any bets?" The dog chose that moment to let out a joyful bark, and all three of them laughed. Then Owen navigated back to the search page and keyed in Sir Corbyn's name, along with the terms *World War II* and *hospital*.

Frowning, and suddenly famished, Robyn

grabbed her slice of pizza and nibbled on the end of it while wondering where he was heading with this.

"Ah-ha!" Owen let out a whoop as he pointed at the first search result, clicking to the webpage before either woman could read what was on the screen.

There, before them, was a series of photos of a beautiful English country manor house, some black-and-white, some more current. The house was gray stone and sprawling, with turrets and gables, and a lush, rolling yard lined with rose bushes of every color variety bursting with life.

Robyn let out a soft, involuntary moan of longing as she studied the photos; the place looked like something out of a fairy tale. "Sir Corbyn actually *lived* here?" she said with a sigh.

"Looks like this is *one* of his houses." Owen clicked on one of the black-and-white photos to enlarge it. The man from the earlier photograph stood in front of it alongside a 1930s-era car and a diminutive woman with a severe face and hair pulled back tightly in a bun. "He and his wife, Cornelia, stayed here during the summer. It's in Cheshire, so not too far from the coast."

He continued scrolling down the page, stopping at another black-and-white photograph, this one showing nurses in neat uniforms tending to rows of wounded soldiers lying in beds.

Catching on, Robyn inhaled sharply. "This house was used as a hospital, then?"

Owen nodded. "One of many throughout the country that opened its doors to soldiers in need. Many of them remained operational throughout the war, and they tended to the wounded and dying when the larger hospitals were either overflowing or too far for transport. Given how costly World War II was in terms of casualties, it would have been a constantly rotating door of patients. John was a soldier and"—he sat back triumphantly and grabbed his slice of pizza for the first time—"I'm willing to bet good money that Rosie was one of his nurses." He grinned at Robyn, then took an enormous bite.

"So you think John and Rosie were both British?" Brooke asked, elbowing Owen out of the way so she could take her turn in front of the laptop. As she gazed at the faces of the many soldiers receiving treatment, the light in her eyes dimmed. "How awful this must have been."

The three of them remained silent for a few moments after that, each lost in their own thoughts of the many lives lost so many years ago, until Owen cleared his throat and said, "Not necessarily."

"Not necessarily what?" Robyn turned her attention away from the laptop and swallowed the lump of emotion in her throat.

"They weren't necessarily British." Owen leaned back into the cushion and, still holding his paper plate in one hand, raked his free hand through his hair. "These makeshift hospitals would have been available to any Allied soldier in need, not to mention any prisoners of war who required care. And while most of the nurses who tended to the soldiers were probably British, they could have come from any friendly country who provided medical aide to England. I think I read once that the United States sent something like sixty thousand nurses alone to Europe and the Pacific during this time. So..." He shrugged, looking pained.

"Rosie and John could have literally come from anywhere," Brooke finished, groaning as she slumped back against the couch. "All this information, and we're no better off now than we were when we started."

"That's not necessarily true," Robyn said. She had pulled the laptop closer and was scrolling down the webpage detailing Sir Corbyn's contribution to the war effort. "We might just be in luck," she said, jabbing her pizza slice at the very bottom of the page. "It says here that this house—they call it Highmont Manor—has been turned into a museum and visitors center. Given its historical significance, Sir Corbyn, upon his death, bequeathed it to the government. It's become a historic landmark."

"How does that help us?" Brooke asked with a frown. Robyn noticed that she was sitting shoulder to shoulder with Owen, but neither of them bothered to shift away.

"We could call them," Robyn suggested. "See if they have any records left over from the time—lists of soldiers who were treated there, maybe, or even the nurses. If we could get that..." Her voice trailed off as she considered the implications. "I mean, how many Rosies could have been there? If we can get our hands on that information, we'll probably have the answer to the mystery of Rosie and John in no time."

Brooke started to look excited, but Owen shook his head. "I don't think it's going to be that easy," he cautioned. "Record-keeping during the war was scattered at best—how could it not be, with the sheer volume of casualties that happened on a daily basis? Not to mention nurses being rotated in and out of various hospitals..."

He sighed and reached out to pat Duke's head.

"I'm just not sure this is the magic bullet we're looking for."

Robyn felt some of her own excitement ebbing too, but she shook her head resolutely. "I'm choosing to be optimistic—this *will* lead us to Rosie."

She propped one foot on the coffee table and reached for a can of soda, popping the tab and taking a long swallow as she scanned the text on the screen once more, noticing for the first time the contact information for the Highmont Manor at the very bottom of the page.

The museum was closed now, but…

"Tomorrow," she said with a grin, raising her can of soda and clinking it against Owen's. "I'm going to call them tomorrow."

CHAPTER 10

The next morning dawned cloudy, with a brisk, unseasonably biting wind whipping up off the ocean, but Robyn didn't mind. Stepping out onto her back patio, and gazing up at the forested mountains shrouded in mist beneath a steely sky, had left her enchanted enough to grab her camera and snap a few photos with the vague idea of sending them off to Coastal Publications for inclusion in some future magazine issue. She'd been in touch with editor-in-chief Melody a handful of times since arriving on Thistle Island, but so far, the assignments she'd been handed had been less than exciting.

Jacket wrapped around herself, steaming mug of tea by her side, Robyn sat at the small wrought-iron table overlooking the patch of grass that constituted her backyard before the scenery rose up into the heavens, and typed out a few listless ideas for the "Modern Bachelor Party Ideas" article she was slated to pen for the next issue of *Coastal Weddings*. Every so often, she glanced at the time on her phone and did a quick mental calculation to determine when the Highmont Manor would be opening for the day—early afternoon in Cheshire, meaning mid-morning for her, and she'd determined long ago that the minutes couldn't have ticked by any more slowly if they tried.

She kept Rosie's latest love letter to John on the table beside her for inspiration as she worked, stopping every few minutes to gaze up at the misty sky and wonder whether either of them was still out there somewhere, waiting to be reunited. Perhaps by her.

At that last thought, Robyn shook her head and let out a soft sigh of regret. Wishful thinking, she knew, but it was nice to envision *someone* having a happy ending. Even if it wasn't her.

With that in mind, and her stomach in knots, she glanced at the phone—though this time, not at the clock. Instead, she flicked up on the screen and navigated to her text messages, where Keith's waited, still unanswered. She hesitated, fingers flexing with indecision, and then glanced once more at the bottle, at the message of lost love entombed within.

How are you doing?

She tapped the words out quickly, then hit "send" before she could reconsider. Before she could remind herself that the man on the other end of that message could never truly offer her the things she wanted, the things she craved, as important to her as oxygen.

As important to her as John was to Rosie.

She heard the grass rustling behind her and turned to find Levi's daughter edging up the yard toward her, smiling shyly, looking unsure whether she was welcome.

"Delaney!" Robyn said, genuinely delighted to see her. "Are you stopping by to say hello?"

It was only then that she noticed the little girl had set a bag at her feet and was glancing between it and Robyn with an uncertain expression. "What's all this?" she asked, crossing the yard to her and peering inside to find several smooth gray stones and pots of paint in bright colors.

"Stepping stones." Delaney bent down and retrieved one of the stones, holding it out to Robyn. "You said yesterday that I could come over and paint some with you?" Her eyes were impossibly wide, eternally hopeful, and Robyn felt her heart squeeze with affection for the little girl.

"Of course!" she said, accepting the stone and turning it over in her hands. "But I thought... your father..." She chewed on her bottom lip, unsure how to approach the thorny subject of Levi with his daughter. Finally, she settled on, "Did your dad say it was okay for you to come here?"

"Oh, yes." The little girl beamed. "He's coming too! He said he'll be here in a minute and that we should get started without him."

"He's... coming?" Robyn echoed, trying her best to hide the horror she was certain was painted all over her face. What had sounded like a charming activity now seemed rather... unpleasant. Sure, she and Levi had come to some sort of an understanding yesterday—at least she *thought* they did—and now, after her conversation with Brooke, she had a better grasp of the man behind the gruff exterior, but that didn't mean she wanted the two of them to be bosom buddies.

Or any kind of buddies at all.

Fortunately, Delaney was too busy opening up the paints and brushes and arranging them on the patio table to notice Robyn's sudden lack of enthusiasm, so she did her best to push those feelings aside. She headed for the kitchen instead, returning with paper cups of fresh water for dipping paintbrushes into, and a plate of brownies she'd baked last night that had Delaney squealing with delight, before they both settled down in the chairs just as the first rays of the sun broke through the morning gloom.

Robyn sat back, considering her stepping stone for a few moments, but Delaney immediately got to work, tongue peeking out from between her lips as she dipped her brush into the cobalt-blue paint, swirled it around, and lowered it, dripping, onto her stone. Then she added streaks of pale pink and deep purple, blending them with flourishes and twirls of her brush.

"What are you painting?" Robyn asked, leaning forward to watch the little girl at work.

"The sky," she said, pursing her lips as her brush hovered over the paints, undecided. Finally, she chose white and added a few puffy clouds to the scene. "It reminds me of my mom."

"Oh, really?" Robyn asked, reaching for a cheerful yellow color with the idea of painting a few sunflowers. Her artistry left plenty to be desired, though, and they ended up looking more like fat suns. She eyed them, then, shrugging, rotated the stone so that they were now in the sky and added several brushstrokes around each for rays, choosing to ignore the fact that no sky on this planet boasted multiple suns. "Do you remember anything about your mom?"

The question was silly, of course; Robyn knew from what Brooke had told her that Delaney's mother had died when she was a newborn. Still, she sensed the girl wanted to talk about Sara, and perhaps didn't want to do it around her father.

"Nope." Delaney plunged her brush into the cup of water, immediately turning it a deep, murky brown. "But my daddy says she's always looking down on me, so I like to think she lives in the sky."

Robyn had no response to that; she was too busy trying to unclog her throat from the lump that had formed inside. "Oh," was all she managed to squeak out, but the little girl seemed not to notice. Then she turned her pretty hazel eyes on Robyn and said, "Do *you* have a mother?"

"Well, sure." Robyn opted to paint a light blue sky, followed by several V-shaped birds soaring toward the sun… well, suns. "Everyone has a mother. But I guess mine lives in the sky now, too."

With a pang, she pictured her mother's face, laughing, carefree, the way she chose to remember her. The resemblance between her and her sister Claire was uncanny; Robyn had mostly taken after her father. Another pang as she recalled their argument, wondered once more whether she was being too stubborn, too unyielding, over his new relationship.

Delaney sighed. "I wish mine was here, living with me and my dad." She cocked her head, her black hair cascading over her shoulders. "Do you wish yours was here too?"

"Every day." Robyn swallowed hard. "Every single day."

The little girl nodded, seeming satisfied with that response, and then returned to her work, now painting a green house that resembled her own. Robyn's enthusiasm had ebbed somewhat; she sat staring at the stepping stone without actually seeing it, too busy imagining what it must have been like for her father, puttering around that sprawling Victorian house of her childhood all on his own, listening for the sound of her mother's voice or her laughter ringing through the halls that would never come.

"You aren't painting." Delaney's voice was almost accusatory as she furrowed her brows in Robyn's direction, and Robyn immediately, obediently, picked up her paintbrush, her lips turned up in a soft smile. Just then, she heard the rustle of grass and glanced up to find Levi crossing the yard toward them. He wasn't wearing his wide-brimmed hat this time, leaving his dark, wavy hair on full display, and she realized as he approached them that his hazel eyes were the exact same shade as his daughter's.

And no less stunning.

"Hi," he said, smiling down at them. The expression brought new life to his face, softening the hard planes and angles and highlighting the laugh lines around his mouth and eyes. "Mind if I sit?" He directed the question at Robyn, who immediately waved him into an empty chair.

"Pull up a stepping stone and join us," she said, reaching into the bag at Delaney's feet and passing him one of the stones. When she handed it to him, their fingers grazed, and she pulled back automatically.

Noticing this, he frowned, eyes downcast for a few moments, before he raised his gaze to hers and said, "I owe you an apology."

The words were so sincere that Robyn waved her hand in the air and said, "No, don't worry about—"

"Yes. I do." His voice was firm. Then he sighed and ran his fingers idly down the dark stubble on his cheeks. "I was out of line. It might seem like a silly, trivial thing to you, but that bedspread, those curtains… they represent a memory to me, a time in my life I can never get back. And even though many years have passed since then, I'm still protective over them. The memories, I mean."

"I understand. Consider it forgotten." Robyn reached across the table and rested her fingers lightly on his wrist. He began to recoil from her touch but stopped himself and drew a deep breath, then released it on a sigh.

"Thank you," he said. Then, as if realizing for the first time that Delaney was sitting there—although still fully engrossed in her work, now adding a dog to the scene along with a scattering of trees—he leaned over and kissed the top of her head. When he withdrew from her, he sat back, arms crossed over his chest, and stared at his blank stone before letting his eyes wander over to Robyn's own masterpiece.

"Is that… four suns?" he asked, eyebrows shooting up into his hairline.

"It is," she said defiantly. "I'm being whimsical."

"Ah, well then." He nodded once in her direction. "Carry on."

The three of them sat in silence for the next few minutes, broken only by the swish of their paintbrushes in water and the occasional munching of a brownie—which, Robyn noted with satisfaction, were quickly disappearing. The morning mist hanging over the mountains had largely dissipated, leaving behind a breathtaking view of the towering pine trees climbing into the sky. Behind them, she could hear the gentle lapping of the ocean against the shore, and the flapping of sails in the wind as boats prepared to launch out of the harbor. Even Levi was engrossed in his work, painting an intricate leaf pattern that was surprisingly artistic.

"Show-off," she said to him with a grin, holding up her finished stone, which, admittedly, looked like something a three-year-old could have bested.

Delaney, satisfied with her design, set her stone carefully on the grass in a patch of sunlight to allow it to dry. After a few more sweeps of his brush, Levi did the same, and Robyn had just added hers to the trio when Helen rounded the corner into the backyard, hands on hips, expression severe.

"Thanks for inviting me to the party," she said, then bent over the paintings to study them. A few moments later, she straightened up again, frowning and stroking her chin while shaking her head in confusion. Then she glanced around the yard, as if looking for something.

"What?" Robyn asked, following her gaze.

Helen shrugged. "I was just looking for Duke, Owen's dog, but he must have left already." She pointed at Robyn's stone. "I figure he's the artist responsible for this one."

Then she met Robyn's indignant gaze and burst out laughing. "Stick with your day job, sweets. Which reminds me"—she waved her hand toward the house—"I have a very exciting day planned for us. When's the last time you caught a mouse? I have a nest of them somewhere in the walls and the squeaking's driving me batty. I was up all night on the couch with a baseball bat, waiting for one to run by."

She mimed swinging a bat like a pro baseball player, then, once again catching sight of Robyn's horrified expression, broke out in peals of laughter. "It's too easy." She patted Robyn on the hand. "I'm beginning to think I'm too much for you to handle, dear."

"You're too much for *anyone* to handle." Levi glanced up from the table, where he and Delaney were packing up the paints. The little girl had streaks on her nose and cheeks, and her shirt looked like it had been tie-dyed.

Robyn stared at him. Did she just hear him crack a joke?

"So." Helen nodded toward the bottle containing Rosie's latest message, which Robyn had set carefully in the grass. "What's the scuttlebutt? You and your new friends make any progress on Thistle Island's greatest mystery?"

"We did," Robyn said, and then proceeded to fill the older woman in on what she, Owen, and Brooke had learned about Sir Corbyn the previous night. Even Levi looked interested in what they had dug up, leaning against the table and listening intently while Robyn described the makeshift war hospital that Corbyn had allowed to occupy his Cheshire home.

"Well I'll be darned," Helen said, looking impressed when Robyn had finished. "The three of you might actually be on to something. So what's next?"

"I'm going to call Highmont Manor this morning and see if I can get someone to speak to me about their history," Robyn said, glancing at the time on her phone. She had been so engrossed in her painting—and enjoyed Delaney's and, yes, even Levi's company so much—that she hadn't realized the museum had been open for over an hour. "Actually, I'm going to call them right now."

She snatched her phone off the table, then waved goodbye to Levi and Delaney and promised Helen she'd be over soon to help her with the laundry and dusting before slipping back inside her bungalow. There, she made a beeline for the kitchen table, where she'd left the notes she'd taken the previous night, along with the museum's contact information.

"It's time to find out who you are," she said to the bottle, which she'd set on the table beside her notes. She reached out to run her fingers along the cork one last time, trying to picture the woman who had slipped the letter inside and sent it off into the swirling sea, before dialing the museum's number and holding her breath while she waited for someone to answer.

"Highmont Manor," a pleasant-sounding woman answered a few moments later. "This is Isabelle speaking, how may I direct your call?"

"Hi," Robyn said. "My name is Robyn Wright, and I was hoping to speak to someone who might be knowledgeable about the manor's role as a hospital during the Second World War."

She launched into a brief explanation of the messages that had washed to shore over the years, and when she had finished, Isabelle said, "That's fascinating, Ms. Wright. I run the museum's gift shop, so unfortunately I'm not able to assist you, but we do have a historian on staff—his name is Bernard Filch, and I'm sure he'd loved to speak with you further about this. Please hold for one moment and I'll redirect your call to him."

Robyn thanked her and waited, drumming her fingertips on the tabletop as she listened to the classical music drifting over the line. The minutes ticked by, and Robyn was just beginning to shift impatiently in her chair and debate hanging up when the line clicked and a softspoken man greeted her and introduced himself as the manor's historian.

Robyn immediately launched into her explanation again—by now, she was beginning to feel like a broken record—and when she was finished, he let out a long, low whistle, and said, "What a beautiful story. Yes, you are indeed correct that Highmont Manor served as a hospital for our brave men and women who were injured during the war, and your friend—Owen, did you say his name was?—is also correct that our record-keeping at that time was spotty at best. The country—and indeed the entire world—was in constant turmoil, and oftentimes the soldiers being brought in for care had no identification with them."

Bernard sighed. "Sadly, many of them also died without anyone even knowing their names. We have a cemetery for the unknown soldiers on our grounds that is open for our visitors to walk through—it's in a beautiful, tree-lined meadow, and I visit there often myself, always hoping the men who were laid to rest there have found peace."

He cleared his throat, and Robyn found herself blinking back tears. "Given that, and how common the name is to begin with, I'm afraid that identifying John with any kind of accuracy would be quite impossible," he concluded.

Robyn nodded along, having expected this response. "But what about Rosie?" she said. "Were there any records of the nurses who were sent to work at the hospital?"

Bernard was quiet for a long moment. When he finally spoke, he said, "You're making an assumption, of course, that Rosie was a nurse. The manor might have been a makeshift hospital, but it was fully functioning in many ways—in addition to the medical staff, there were housekeepers, cooks, orderlies… some of them employed, some of them volunteers. Many of Cheshire's residents who wanted to do their part for the war effort dedicated their time to the hospital and may have come into contact with the patients. So you see, your Rosie could have been…"

"Anyone." Robyn finished the sentence for him, disappointment settling over her. "She could have been absolutely anyone."

There was another long pause, followed by a soft exhalation of breath. "Yes," Bernard said. "I'm afraid that's correct. However." He hesitated, apparently in thought, and Robyn could feel her fingers tightening on the phone. "You may have one or two options left to pursue, although it's entirely possible they won't amount to anything."

"That's okay." Robyn grabbed a pad of paper and pen from the kitchen counter and balanced the phone between ear and shoulder, preparing to jot down his next words. "What can you tell me?"

Bernard cleared his throat. "This is working off the assumption that Rosie *was* a nurse, which is entirely possible. In fact, I'd go a step further and venture to say it's probable. The medical staff would have had the most direct contact with the soldiers, and if Rosie and John met while he was convalescing at the Highmont Manor, he would have had more regular access to nurses than anyone else—other than, of course, the soldiers in the neighboring beds, although I highly doubt one of them was named Rosie."

He laughed softly, then his voice grew somber again. "Nurses were in high demand during the war, of course, but even decades before then, Great Britain had the foresight to establish a medical unit that provided nursing services to our forces stationed around the world. This was known by the rather cumbersome name of Queen Alexandria's Imperial Military Nursing Service." He chuckled. "That sounds quite official, does it not?"

"It does," Robyn agreed, brow furrowed deeply as she wrote down the name.

"It started off small," Bernard continued, "with only a few hundred nurses at the start of the First World War. By 1918, that number had ballooned to ten thousand. They served bravely in every campaign of the war, and they brought great comfort to our wounded and dying men. Some of them even gave up their lives to protect our country. In the Second World War, they were called to service again, and again they carried out their duties bravely and admirably."

"So what you're saying," Robyn interjected, trying

to keep up, "is that Rosie may have been one of the women serving in this unit."

"Correct," Bernard confirmed, "and if so, you are in luck."

"How so?" she asked eagerly, setting down her pen and listening hard.

"Because she will have been considered a member of the military, and thus her name will be included in the records our government maintained—and still maintains—in the National Archives. This is a searchable database, and you can access it from anywhere—including right from your own home across the pond, as we like to say."

There was a smile in his voice, and Robyn automatically mirrored the expression as a feeling of excitement welled up within her. She couldn't wait to tell Owen—okay, *boast* to Owen—that Rosie's identity might be right here, at their fingertips, before the end of the day.

"And the second option?" Robyn asked, imagining the looks on her new friends' faces when she delivered the good news.

"A little less of a sure thing in terms of record-keeping, I'm afraid, but still a worthwhile path to follow. Give me one moment to make sure I have the details correct…"

She could hear him typing on a keyboard in the background, then mumbling quietly to himself before saying, "Ah, yes, here we go. St. George's Nursing School is one of the largest nursing programs in all of England, and it was operational at the time of the Second World War—and more significantly, I hope, is that it was located right here in Cheshire, only two miles from Highmont Manor. During the war years, the school sent many of their nurses-in-training to assist the medical staff here at the manor. I'm not sure what records remain, if any, of their students from that time, but I believe it would be worth your while to call their offices and see if they'd be willing to give you any more information. I have their number here…"

He rattled off a telephone number and Robyn scrawled it down, her excitement mounting. Now they had two good options for identifying Rosie—and she could feel it in her bones that one of them would lead her in the right direction.

Just then her phone chimed with an incoming text, and she pulled it away from her ear to see Keith's response to her earlier impulsive message flash across the screen.

Missing you like crazy. Can't eat, can't sleep. Can we meet? Please.

And just like that, she was pulled back into the present. Back into the heartache and the uncertainty and the fear that she was doing the wrong thing.

Or was it the fear that she was doing the *right* thing?

She stared at the phone for a few seconds, stomach churning, heart in her throat, until she heard the sound of Bernard's tinny voice and realized he had begun talking again. Hurriedly, she brought the phone to her ear just in time to hear him say, "I do hope this has helped. If there's anything else I can do for you, please let me know. And if you find the time, I'd love to hear how it all plays out."

"Me too," Robyn said softly, her mind still on Keith's words. "I'd love to hear how it all plays out too."

CHAPTER 11

"Move *over*." Brooke elbowed Owen out of the way and drew her chair closer to the laptop. "Just because you're a history teacher doesn't mean you get first dibs on Rosie. Why don't you go read a book on ancient toilets or something."

"Now *that's* a fascinating subject," Owen said, his entire face lighting up as he obligingly pushed his chair aside to make room for her. "Did you know that the first flushing toilets were developed four thousand years ago? They were discovered in a palace on the island of Crete in the Mediterranean, however some scholars argue that it was *actually* the Indus Valley Civilization in present-day Pakistan that can boast about having the first flushable—"

"If I hear one more fact about toilets, I'm going to stick your head in one," Brooke interrupted, her green eyes flashing dangerously. When Owen tossed a wounded look her way—the resemblance to Duke pining after a pizza was uncanny, Robyn decided—she softened automatically, her lips curving into a smile. "Okay, fine, that *may* have been a little harsh. But seriously, Owen, what's wrong with you?"

When he opened his mouth, she held up a hand. "Don't answer that." Then she leaned forward and kissed him lightly on the cheek. "You know I love you, but I'd love you even more if you shut your pie hole and let me focus on this."

As she refocused on the computer screen in front of her, Robyn noticed Owen's fingers drifting to the spot where Brooke's lips had just been, his eyes on her face. When he caught Robyn watching him, he smiled, dropped his hand to his lap, and scooted his chair forward so he could join the two women in front of the laptop.

The three of them were huddled around Robyn's kitchen table, rapidly cooling mugs of coffee at their sides, platter of sandwiches she had thrown together left untouched. After ending her conversation with Bernard, she had immediately called them, and both had promised to be at her house within the hour.

They had arrived together, barely containing their enthusiasm as she promptly led them into the kitchen while reviewing everything Bernard had told her about Highmont Manor and its role in the war. Now they were preparing to access the UK's National Archives, and Robyn could feel the excitement thrumming in the air around them as a tangible force.

Brooke navigated to the archives website and had just found the search bar to access individual military records when they were interrupted by a firm knock at the door. "Who could that be?" Robyn murmured, glancing out the kitchen window at Helen's house with a frown. The older woman was enjoying lunch with several of her friends today in town, and Robyn wasn't due to pick her up for another two hours, giving her the perfect window of time to make progress on the mystery of Rosie.

Then she caught sight of her phone lying innocently on the kitchen counter and her heart stalled. She hadn't answered Keith's message yet—and had no idea what she would say when she did—but what if he had decided to forgo formalities and appear on her doorstep? Lump of panic in her throat, she mentally calculated the time between his last message and how long it would take him to drive to Thistle Island…

And the math worked out perfectly.

"Are you okay?" Brooke was peering at her in concern, and even Owen had torn his eyes away from the computer to study her face. "You look a little… nauseated." She tossed a glare Owen's way. "It was probably all that toilet talk. It's perfectly uncivilized, Owen. Can't you see that Robyn is a lady? But *you're* no gentleman."

He opened his mouth defensively, but another knock on the door stopped him in his tracks. "Expecting company?" Brooke asked, then glanced between the door and Robyn and, noting her suddenly pale face, said softly, sympathetically, "*Oh. You don't think it's him, do you?*" She nudged Owen in the side. "Come on, we better give her some space."

"Who's him?" Owen looked from one woman to the other in bewilderment, but Brooke merely gave him a curt shake of her head and steered him toward the back door, out onto the patio. On the way back from Owen's house the previous night, Robyn had given her a brief, painful explanation of the reason she had decided to move to Thistle Island—including the implosion of her decade-long relationship with Keith—and Brooke had listened with a sympathetic ear. And while she appreciated her thoughtfulness right now, if Keith really was standing on Robyn's front porch, she didn't need space.

She needed backup.

Because she had no idea if she was strong enough to face him without breaking down completely. Or worse, throwing herself into his arms and forgetting all the reasons she had left in the first place.

On her way to the door, Robyn caught sight of her stricken face in the hallway mirror and took a moment to arrange her features into a cool, calm, and composed expression that was completely at odds with her inner turmoil. Then, with a deep breath, she pulled the door open.

And there was a man standing on the other side. Just not the one she'd expected.

"Levi!" His name came out in a breath of relief that had him raising his eyebrows in confusion. "What a wonderful surprise!" And she genuinely meant it. An amorous baboon could have been on the other side of that door and she would have welcomed it with open arms. "Come in, come in!" She snaked her hand around his wrist and practically yanked him into the house.

Once over the threshold, he stared at her, running one hand down his stubbled cheek, and then said, "Happy to see me?"

Robyn could feel her cheeks reddening, but she quickly covered the embarrassing moment with a grin and a flippant, "Always. What brings you here?" She glanced down the hall toward the bathroom. "The toilet's been working fine ever since you fixed it, so thanks for that."

"Good, good." Levi nodded and tucked his hands into the pockets of his jeans. They were stained with dirt and grass, and the bottom of his boots looked like he'd recently been tramping through mud. Noticing her eyes on them, he removed them and set them neatly outside the front door, then said, "This is actually a social call, if it's okay with you. I saw Owen's car out front and thought you two might be working on that message in a bottle you found."

"We are," Robyn said in surprise. "I didn't know you were all that interested in Rosie and John."

"As much as anybody, I guess," he said with a one-shoulder shrug. "But I've got the day off and Delaney's out with a friend for the afternoon, so I figured…" He studied her face, looking noticeably uncomfortable, then gestured out the door. "I can leave, if you want. I don't mean to intrude."

"You aren't intruding! And we'd love for you to stay—the more, the merrier. Owen's here, and Brooke too." As she was speaking, she led him down the bungalow's short hallway toward the kitchen. "You have good timing. We were just about to begin our search."

Indicating the fourth chair around the table, she said, "Sit," and grabbed him a plate. "Eat." She waved one hand toward the sandwiches. "I made enough for an army, but no one's taken a single bite. I'm starting to think my sandwich-making skills leave a lot to be desired."

"Looks good to me," Levi said, helping himself to a turkey and Swiss on rye. He devoured it in a few bites—*inhaled* may have been a better word—and then grabbed a second, starting in on it immediately.

Robyn watched him, one eyebrow raised in amusement. "Don't you ever eat at your place?"

Levi swallowed a mouthful of ham and cheddar, then laughed—a deep, booming laugh that Robyn immediately liked. "Oh, we eat plenty, believe me. But I've been cooking for myself for the past seven years, and food just tastes better when someone else prepares it."

"Amen to that." She pulled out the chair beside him and plonked into it. "I was the cook in my house, too. My boy—" She pursed her lips and gave him a rueful smile. "My *ex*-boyfriend couldn't quite get the hang of it. The man could burn a peanut butter and jelly sandwich."

A stab of pain at the memory—the two of them standing in the kitchen, heads thrown back with laughter, him holding the charred piece of toast in one hand and a butter knife in the other, intent on scraping off the burned areas. When the image faded, she forced a smile, but even she could tell it was less than convincing.

Levi gave her a searching look. "You been single for long?"

She opened her mouth to answer but was interrupted by the back door banging open and Brooke and Owen emerging from the patio. "We heard laughter, so we figured it was okay for us to come—"

Brooke stopped speaking when she reached the kitchen doorway and found Robyn and Levi sitting at the table. "Well, well, *well*, what have we here?" She slid a meaningful glance Robyn's way, but it was gone in a flash as she crossed the room to Levi and bent down to wrap her arms around him.

"As I live and breathe, if it isn't Levi Graham. I was starting to think you had become a hermit. How are you, honey?" She released him and straightened, smiling down at him. "We've missed seeing you around." Pulling out the chair beside him, she lowered herself into it and grabbed the laptop. "Here to help us put our detective skills to use?"

"I thought I might lend a hand." Levi's gaze snagged on Robyn's for a split second, and they both glanced away. "As long as four isn't a crowd."

"Four isn't a crowd, it's a *party*." Brooke gave him a soft smile as Owen greeted Levi with a bear hug and then dropped into the seat beside Robyn. "Where's Delaney girl? I miss her sweet face."

"On the mainland for a few hours," Levi said, leaning back in his chair and stretching out his long legs beside the table. "Clothes shopping with a friend and her mom." He shuddered slightly. "Glad to have someone else to help me with that, if I'm being honest. The girl's seven years old going on twenty-two, at least if she had it her way. Some of the things she picks up off the rack are enough to stop a father's heart."

He said the words in a playful tone, but Robyn immediately caught the undercurrent of sadness in them. It struck her once again how difficult being a single father must be, especially to a young girl. They would have to navigate plenty of thorny times ahead, times when Delaney would acutely and painfully miss the mother she'd never known.

"If you ever need help with something like that, I'd be glad to give you a hand." Robyn said the words without thinking, and Brooke and Owen regarded her with surprise.

Levi, however, fixed his hazel eyes on hers and nodded once, a look of understanding passing between them. "I appreciate the offer, and I might take you up on it someday. Thank you."

Another shared look, this one slightly less awkward than before, and in that moment, a sudden realization dawned on Robyn.

She was starting to like Levi. Not in *that* way, but... she could see them becoming actual friends someday. For some strange reason, the thought had her heart feeling lighter.

Brooke snuck her another side-eyed look, then turned her attention back to the laptop, rubbing her hands together and saying, "Now, back to our regularly scheduled program. Should I do the honors?" She had pulled open the website for the archives again and navigated to the tab to search for individual war records before crossing her fingers. "Here's to hoping there weren't a thousand women named Rosie in the nursing corps." Then she lowered her hands to the keyboard and began to type.

Robyn held her breath, and beside her, she could sense Owen doing the same. He was leaning forward eagerly, his face boyish with anticipation, his blue eyes scanning the webpage as Brooke keyed in "Rosie" and hit the enter button.

No search results.

Robyn groaned out loud, but Owen merely shook his head and said, "Keep trying. We need to come up with every possible name that could have Rosie as a shortened version or nickname. Rose, Rosamund, Rosalie, Rosa, Rosalina…"

Brooke was feverishly typing names into the database, each time coming up empty. On the last try, the name Rosalina pulled up a positive identity, and Owen actually let out a whoop of exhilaration.

Until, that is, they saw that the name belonged to Edward Rosalina, a soldier killed in the Battle of the Bulge.

"Nothing." Brooke ran a frustrated hand through her hair. "I was *sure* we would find something."

"We still have another option," Robyn said, trying to keep her voice upbeat. "I'm going to place a call to St. George's Nursing School and see if we can get a list of alumni who attended the school in the 1930s or early 1940s. But…" She hesitated, not wanting to voice her fears out loud.

"But what?" Owen prompted, looking personally affronted that the archives had let him down.

Robyn exhaled, long and loud. "Something you said, about Rosie being a nickname? What if it was… for an entirely different name. For all we know, her name could have really been Catherine. What then?"

The four of them fell silent at that, with Brooke looking especially crestfallen. Then Levi leaned forward and said in a quiet voice, "Then Rosie and John remain a mystery. Maybe it's what they would have wanted, anyway. Their own private love story."

It was a beautiful thought, immediately drawing tears to Brooke's eyes. "Maybe we should stop," she said, dabbing at her eyes with her fingertips. "Levi has a point, you know. We're trying to force something here for our own curiosity… but if Rosie wanted to be found, maybe someone would have found her already."

"Someone may have," Owen pointed out. "We have no idea where these bottles originated, and how many were sent. For all we know, Rosie *did* identify herself in one of them. Or someone else got as curious as us and tracked her down. Given the time period we're talking about, this could have happened years ago. Decades, even."

The others were nodding along, and even though Robyn understood their point, that didn't stop the knots forming in the pit of her stomach. She needed this right now. Something to focus on, something to keep her mind from spinning its endless web of *what ifs*. Something to stop her from picking up that phone and calling Keith, accepting his request to talk things out.

She needed to know that true love—the kind that lasted beyond death—really did exist, and that she still had a chance of finding it someday.

Robyn pushed back her chair, the sound like a gunshot in the silence that had descended over the group. Three pairs of eyes watched her as she made a beeline for the kitchen counter to grab the notes she'd taken during her earlier conversation with Bernard, and then to her phone.

She had a call to make.

CHAPTER 12

Much to Robyn's disappointment, the nursing school in Cheshire was closed for the day, so she left a message with the director of alumni relations and silently prayed that someone would reach out to her soon. Then she said goodbye to Owen, Brooke, and Levi and headed into town to pick Helen up from the café where she and her friends were having lunch.

"You're awfully quiet," Helen said on the car ride back, watching Robyn from the corner of her eye. "Got a bee in your bonnet?" They came to a crosswalk, slowing to a stop to allow a mother and her two young children to cross the road, sand pails in hand and beach towels streaming behind them like flags, the ends fluttering in the breeze blowing in from the water.

The misty morning had given way to a glorious afternoon, with a cerulean sky that swept over a softly rippling dark blue ocean. A lone seagull dipped in and out of the single puffy cloud floating low over the water, and on the horizon, a row of sailboats bobbed in the gentle waves. The shoreline was dotted with colorful umbrellas, chairs, and coolers as day-vacationers and residents alike enjoyed the early-summer warmth.

Even though outside the scenery was beautiful, and serene, and picturesque, on the inside, Robyn felt the weight of sadness settling over her like a shroud. "Can I ask you something?" she asked, turning in her seat to face Helen. Behind her, the coastal road was clear of cars.

"What's on your mind, girlie?" Helen's light eyes roved over Robyn's face, gently scrutinizing her.

"Do you believe in true love?"

It was a simple question, so why were Robyn's eyes suddenly wet with tears? A single one trailed down her cheek and landed in her lap, darkening the fabric of her jeans.

"That's a loaded question." Helen glanced behind them, then gestured for Robyn to navigate the car to a small, four-space parking lot adjacent to the beach. The older woman waited until they were parked before she removed her glasses and squeezed her eyes shut, pinching her nose with forefinger and thumb and sighing heavily.

"I'm sorry," Robyn said quietly, already regretting the question. "That's a pretty personal thing to ask. Just… let's forget about it, okay?"

Helen leaned across the center console and patted her leg. "What good are friends if you can't ask them a personal question or two? And to answer your original question…" She inhaled softly, then let the breath out on a sigh. "Yes. I do believe in true love, but I also think it takes many forms, beyond the romantic kind."

She gazed out the window; the mother and children who had crossed the road were now on their knees in the sand, hair blowing in their mouths, laughing as they dug a hole and filled it with seawater. "I've never been blessed with children of my own," she said in a quiet voice, "but from what I've seen, that kind of love—the kind a mother has for her little ones—might be the most powerful one of all. And I think we can find true love with our friends, too, and even the place where we live." She let her hand dangle out the window, toward the ocean. "The relationship I have with this island is just as powerful as the relationships I've had with people I've known throughout my lifetime. In some cases, even more so."

"But the romantic kind?" Robyn pressed, needing to know the answer but not quite understanding why. Maybe it was because Helen had been around long enough to see things, to understand things, to gain the type of wisdom that Robyn was still seeking.

Maybe it was because she wanted someone to tell her that there was still hope.

Helen lifted her head, her gaze tracking a flock of birds soaring out over the open water. "Oh yes," she said. "Yes, I very much believe in the romantic kind of true love, the idea of soulmates. And when we find it, we need to hold onto it with everything we have."

"But what if we don't find it?" Another tear tracing a path down her cheek; another dark patch on her jeans. "Or worse yet, what if we found it but didn't recognize it? What if we let it go?"

Helen was quiet for a long moment after that. Robyn dried her tears; a seagull outside the window landed beside the car and peered at her with blazing orange eyes, hoping for a scrap of food. When the older woman finally spoke, her voice was nearly carried away amid the sound of the waves crashing to shore.

"I don't have an answer to that—at least not the one I suspect you want. But I've been around for a long time, and I do know this: sometimes our path in life takes us on a journey we never anticipated, maybe never even wanted. Our job is to find our own happiness, to seek peace in what we *do* have, and not in what we don't, or can't, have."

She reached for Robyn's hand, and the two women clung to each other for a moment before Helen pulled away and said, "Don't wish your life away. Take it from someone who knows."

~

Later that night, when the indigo sky was tipped with purple and the sun's last rays had spread over the mountains, highlighting the pine trees in coral and gold, Robyn sat outside on her back porch, mug of hot chocolate in one hand, cell phone in the other. She'd been playing with it for the better part of an hour, picking it up and setting it down, threading it through her fingers, swiping up on the screen only to immediately push the button to darken it again—and all the while, Helen's words played in her mind.

Had she found true love with Keith? For many years, the answer to that question would have been a resounding yes. What had started out as an initial spark of attraction had eventually settled into a familiar, quiet kind of love—a friend to laugh with, a shoulder to cry on in hard times, a hand to hold in joyous ones. He was a good man. A solid man. The type of man many women had been seeking their whole lives.

He wasn't perfect. Who was? Certainly not Robyn.

Missing you like crazy. Can't eat, can't sleep. Can we meet? Please.

Those words had been a heavy weight on her shoulders made heavier by her inability to answer them. She couldn't; she didn't know what to say. She missed him, that much was certain. But truth be told, she *could* eat. She *could* sleep—better than she had in years, in fact.

Sleep, she'd found, had been hard to come by when you never felt quite good enough. When your partnership of a decade balanced on a knife's edge.

Balanced on an ultimatum.

The worst part of it was that he hadn't even taken

her seriously. Hadn't thought for one second that his inability to commit to her had robbed her of some of her worth. She'd had to summon an enormous amount of courage, and self-love, to demand for things to change.

And until she walked out, she would bet her life that he'd never lost a single wink of sleep over her.

True love takes many forms, beyond the romantic kind.

But there *was* someone who loved her. The first man to adore her. And she missed the sound of his laughter, the twinkle in his ocean-blue eyes, the aroma of his blueberry pancakes on a Sunday morning, almost more than she could bear.

She might not have the romantic kind of love in her life right now. And she had to accept the possibility that she might never have it again.

But she did have a different kind of love, the one that would last a lifetime.

Her heart was in her throat as she dialed the familiar number, holding her breath as it rang once, twice, thr—

"Little bird?"

The beloved nickname was a balm to her broken heart.

"Daddy?" Robyn closed her eyes as his soothing presence, even from a distance, washed over her.

"Little bird, I'm so glad to hear from you." Her father's voice was thick with emotion, and relief. "I can't tell you the number of times I picked up the phone to call you, but... I sensed you needed your space. And a little time to process everything."

"I'm sorry, Dad." Robyn made the apology without preamble; they both understood why it was needed. "When I found out about you and Jessie, it was a shock and..." She laughed softly. "I guess I didn't take it very well, did I? But I've come to understand that if she makes you happy, then she must be very special." She took a deep breath, her throat constricting. "I'd like to get to know her, if you'll let me."

Paul Wright was quiet for several long moments before saying quietly, "I'd like that. I'd like that very much." Then he laughed, the sound like a gentle embrace. "I have to say, I didn't enjoy my pancakes very much the last time I made them. How about a do-over? Next Sunday—same time, same place... same company."

Robyn squeezed the phone tighter to her ear, her face splitting into a smile—what felt like the first true one she'd had since that disastrous morning. "It's a date."

～

EARLY THE NEXT MORNING, a shrill ringing had Robyn shooting up from under the covers, hair in disarray, eyes wild as she stared around for the source of the sound. Finally realizing it was her cell phone—although who would call at this ungodly hour, she had no idea—she groped around in the darkness until she found it on her nightstand. Switching on the table lamp, she peered groggily down at the number, which blurred in and out of focus as she tried to regain her bearings.

And then, recognizing it, she was suddenly wide awake, all traces of sleepiness evaporated.

"Hello?" she said breathlessly, answering just before the call clicked over to voicemail.

"Hello, is this Ms. Wright?" The woman's voice was prim yet friendly. "This is Eugenia Lenox from St. George's Nursing School. I received a message from you yesterday—I believe you're seeking a list of our alumni?"

"Yes, that's right." Robyn could practically hear

her heart pounding down the line. "Would it be possible to receive one?"

"Are you interested in setting up a reunion?" Eugenia asked. "Because if so, we already have a reception set up for the thirtieth of July at the Cheshire Inn and Tea Room. I'd have to check and see if we have any more availability—our alumni events are quite popular—but if you give me a moment—"

"Actually, I'm not interested in a reunion," Robyn broke in, not wanting to waste the woman's time. "I'm hoping to find out whether you have retained records from the women who graduated from your school many years ago—probably the 1930s or early 1940s." When Eugenia expressed surprise at the unusual request, Robyn once again launched into an explanation of the letters, and the long-ago love story she was hoping to solve.

When she was finished, Eugenia said, "How lovely. I'd be happy to help—I just need to make sure our records go back that far. We've been in the process of having them digitized—I'm afraid some of the older paper records were lost in a fire several years back. But I *think…*"

Her voice trailed off, replaced by the sound of keystrokes, and Robyn could feel her knuckles draining of color from the death grip she had on the phone.

"Yes, here it is." Eugenia laughed softly. "It's here—all of it. I'm not sure if it will be of any use to you, but if you provide me with an email address, I can have my assistant send the records over to you when she comes back from her break in a few minutes. Shall we say… 1920s, '30s, and '40s, just to be safe?" When Robyn eagerly agreed, she said, "Keep in mind, though, that these are names and graduation years only—to protect our alumni's privacy, we don't give out any personal details, like addresses or phone numbers."

"I can work with that," Robyn said, then rattled off her email address as she leapt off the bed and padded into the kitchen in search of a cup of tea to calm her nerves while she waited. Fortunately, her inbox chimed with a new message less than ten minutes later, and she immediately set down her cup and clicked open the attachment.

As promised, the records began in 1920, and Eugenia's assistant had left a note that she could procure additional names if Robyn didn't find what she was looking for during those years. She was surprised—and pleased—to find that she wouldn't be combing through thousands of alumni names; St.

George's Nursing School must have been relatively small in the early and mid-twentieth century, with only twenty-five students graduating per year.

The document was searchable, but to Robyn's immense disappointment, a quick key-in of "Rose" and related names yielded nothing. She closed her eyes and dropped her head into her hands for a few moments as she came to the realization that, despite her optimism, they might have run out of options for finding the mysterious woman.

Were Rosie and John lost to history? Just another love story, like the countless others that had occurred throughout the ages.

With a sigh—and knowing her efforts were futile—Robyn began reviewing the records line by line, searching for any name that jumped out at her, any nudge in the right direction, any feeling in her bones that *this one* just might be the one.

Then, when she came to the graduates of 1943, her finger stopped on a name, and she did a double-take, her breath catching in her throat, her heart skipping several beats.

She had found her. She had found Rosie.

She laughed out loud in disbelief, then stared at the name again, her eyes roving over each letter, trying to convince herself that what she was seeing was true.

The answer was so simple. And yet nothing she would have ever expected, or dreamed up.

Immediately, she reached for the phone to dial Owen, already imagining his whoop of excitement upon hearing the news.

Then she stopped. Took a deep breath. And closed the laptop.

Owen and Brooke could wait. There was someone else she needed to share the news with first.

CHAPTER 13

Despite the early hour, Helen was crouched over her rose bushes, deadheading the beautiful blooms that burst with life in almost every color of the rainbow, when she saw Robyn approaching. Setting down her pruning shears, she straightened and raised one weathered hand in greeting. "If you're looking for those donuts you didn't eat the other day, you're too late. I had myself a feast last night." She patted her stomach, then made a show of tugging on the waistband of her pants, grunting from the effort.

Robyn laughed, then pulled the older woman into a spontaneous hug. When she released her, Helen patted her cheek, her eyes sweeping over Robyn's face, assessing her. "Don't you look chipper.

Do I want to know what you were doing last night that put a smile like that on your pretty face?"

Smiling, Robyn teased, "Wouldn't you like to know. But I'm not here to talk about my snuggling partner—which, in this case, was a pillow. I'm here because I have news." She took Helen's hands and gave them a squeeze. "I found Rosie."

Helen's eyes widened in surprise. "You don't say? Well, I suppose this calls for a celebration. I made a pitcher of sweet tea last night—why don't you pour us two glasses and meet me on the front porch. I want to hear all about it."

As Helen made her way toward the pair of Adirondack chairs that faced the harbor, where the water glistened in the first hints of a sunrise, Robyn headed for the kitchen, returning a short while later with the glasses of sweet tea and a plate of shortbread cookies. She offered the cookies to Helen, then took several for herself before settling into the chair, tea in hand, and taking a long, refreshing sip. The women were quiet for a moment, the only sounds the soft munching of cookies and the rumble of waves swelling against the shore.

Finally, Robyn turned to Helen and said, "Why didn't you ever tell anyone?"

Helen laughed softly. "Because nobody ever asked me."

Robyn nodded, eyes on Helen's profile; the older woman kept her gaze on the sparkling sea. "We'll keep this between us," she said softly. "No one has to know the truth. Like you said, everyone has a right to their privacy. I didn't mean to overstep my bounds; I had no idea that all of this time and research would lead to your front door. I haven't told anyone, and if you'd like, I can make sure it stays that way."

Helen lifted one hand off the armrest of her chair, palm up, and offered Robyn a shrug. "Maybe it's time for others to know. Maybe it will help me, finally, to heal." A lone tear trickled down her cheek. "Bearing this burden on my own, all these years... it's taken a toll, far more than I ever expected." As she was talking, her fingers were idly stroking the class ring she wore on her right hand.

"You can talk to me about it, if you'd like," Robyn offered tentatively. "But if you'd rather not, I understand."

Several minutes passed in silence after that, both women continuing to gaze out over the harbor. A lone fishing boat was chugging along far offshore, and she could just make out the men on deck raising a net with the day's catch. She imagined they were calling out to each other, but their voices were lost in the wind and waves. Whenever she chanced a glance in Helen's direction, she found the older woman's face was lined with sadness, her eyes not on the scene in front of them but perhaps one from another time, another place, another life.

"I was only nineteen years old when I met him," she said, her voice wavering slightly as she tore her gaze from the water and fixed it on Robyn's face. "Young—too young to be seeing so many awful things. I entered nursing school when I turned eighteen, and in those years, the war years, nurses were in high demand. The program was shortened, with the hopes that we would learn as much as we could, and then many of us would then go on to support the war effort, the troops."

She shook her head then, frowning. "I should back up. You're probably wondering what I was doing in a nursing school in England to begin with." She gestured behind them, toward Levi's house. "That was the home I was born in, the home I grew up in until I was fourteen years old. My father was an American who had served in World War I, and while overseas, he met my mother, a London schoolteacher. They hit it off, and she moved across the ocean to be with him, although she told me later that leaving her home country was a weight she carried with her every day."

Helen sighed, tracing one finger along the rim of her glass. "When I was fourteen and my sister was eleven, our father passed away quite suddenly, and in her grief, our mother wanted nothing to do with this house, this country—they were too much of a reminder of all that she had lost. So she left the house in the care of my father's sister and returned to England with us."

She shook her head. "The culture shock was something, let me tell you. I wanted to come home, I cried every day for months, but eventually, I learned to love England, though I always knew I would return to the States—and Thistle Island—someday. The war took that off the table temporarily, of course, so I decided to enroll in nursing school, do my part for the men and boys who fought so bravely, and who died as heroes beyond measure."

Her voice cracked on those last words, and she shook her head and whispered, "So many beautiful boys lost. So much heartache and tragedy." After taking a moment to compose herself, she went on, "The Highmont Manor began serving as a hospital during my time in nursing school, and upon graduation, our teachers encouraged us to volunteer there, to gain some hands-on experience while also serving our country. That's where I met him. John Sullivan."

She exhaled gently on the name and her expression softened; suddenly, she looked ten years younger. "Oh, he was handsome—six feet tall, broad shoulders, wavy brown hair, and his eyes... they were a pale blue-gray, the most beautiful eyes I'd ever seen. He was an American fighter pilot based on an airfield in the English countryside not far from where I went to school, and he and his fellow pilots were injured in a bombing attack by the German Luftwaffe. He was brought to our hospital for treatment, and assigned to one of my beds, and oh, Robyn, I just fell head over heels for him the first time I saw him."

A gentle smile crossed her face. "Only those who have never experienced love at first sight don't believe in it, because I can tell you, with all my heart and soul, that it exists. It *exists*. As for the nickname Rosie"—she laughed—"Highmont Manor had these beautiful rose bushes all around the grounds, and when they were in bloom, the nurses used to pick them and pin them to the lapels of our uniform. It was a small way to cheer up the wounded men, to bring some beauty back into their lives when they had experienced such horror. That first day John saw me, I was wearing one of those roses in my hair, and he started calling me Rosie. After that, it became our private joke. To John, I was never Helen. I was always Rosie."

A foghorn blared in the distance, and both women turned their eyes back to the water, where the fishing boat was now gliding to shore. They watched the men scramble around the deck for several long moments, preparing the ship for docking, until Helen let out a soft sigh and said, "We were mad about each other. John was at the hospital for a month, and we talked often of marriage. He gave me this"—she stroked the class ring, her fingers tracing the outline of the sapphire in the center—"as a promise that once the war was over, we would be reunited."

She swallowed hard. "A few days before he was about to be released, my mother fell gravely ill. I immediately left to be with her in what turned out to be her final days, but before John and I said our final goodbye, he handed me a slip of paper with his home address in California, where his mother and younger siblings still lived. Then I kissed him, and told him I loved him, and that…" Her voice trailed off for a moment. "That was the last time I ever saw or heard from him again."

"You tried to find him?" Robyn asked, finding her voice for the first time. "After the war?"

Helen laughed. "During the war. After the war. For years—for *decades*—I tried to find him. I wrote letters, I made telephone calls, I even visited the address he gave me." She met Robyn's gaze, her eyes steeped with sadness. "His mother wasn't there, and no one had ever heard the name John Sullivan. It was like he didn't exist. Like he was a ghost, or a figment of my imagination. A wish that would never come true."

She looked out over the water once more. "Eventually, I had turned over every stone, and when I still couldn't find him, or any trace of his family, I started writing those letters and tossing them into the sea. For myself. I knew they would never reach him, of course, but I admit that sometimes, against all odds and all reason... I had hope." Laughing, she added, "So it was only natural that a few of them washed right back up where they started. I've sent out two a month, every month, for..." She tipped her head in thought, her lips moving silently. "Over nine hundred months." Blowing out a soft breath, she whispered, almost to herself, "Can it have really been that long?"

Robyn was silent for a time as she digested everything she had heard. Then, she said softly, "But the letters you wrote, they almost make it sound like you know that he had…" She left the sentence unfinished, not wanting to upset Helen any further.

"Died," she finished in a broken voice. "He must have. Because otherwise, he would have found me." She dabbed at her eyes with a tissue she slid from her pocket, then crumpled it in her fingers and stared down at it. "In my darkest hours, I convinced myself that he was a ghost. It would have been easier to accept that. But I know, I *know*, that he was real, and what we had was real. If he could have come for me, he would have. No one, and nothing, could convince me otherwise."

Her voice drifted off again, and silence fell between them once more. Robyn focused her attention on her glass of tea, eyes blurred with tears, heart aching from everything she had just heard. After a while, Helen let out a soft laugh and said, "You know? I almost feel better, getting that off my chest. Maybe it was time to unburden myself from everything I've been carrying for so long. Maybe it's truly time to let John go, and let his soul rest in peace, wherever he may be."

"Or maybe it's not." The words were out of Robyn's mouth before she could stop them, and for a moment, she regretted them.

But Helen was looking at her with interest, with... *hope*, and so she pressed on. "We could help you—me, Owen, Brooke, maybe even Levi. There are resources available now that weren't back then. Maybe... maybe we can let John rest knowing that the love of his life finally found him."

At that, Helen fell silent for so long that Robyn feared she had overstepped her bounds. Then, slowly, a beautiful smile graced her face, lighting up her features and stealing Robyn's breath. In that moment, she saw not the old woman who sat beside her but the girl she had been so long ago, when the world was broken but her heart was whole.

Then, eyes clouded with tears, she said, "I think he would like that very much."

Robyn opened her mouth, mind already whirring with possibilities, with paths they could take and stones still left unturned in their search for John, but Helen raised a hand to halt her words and said gently, "I've waited seventy-nine years; believe me when I say I can wait another day. Right now, I think I'd like to just watch the sunrise, and... remember."

She turned her smile to the sky, where a coral sun was sweeping its first rays over the glittering sea, and stretched out her hand for Robyn to take. She held on tight, and together, the two women watched another day on Thistle Island begin anew.

∼

THE STORY CONTINUES in book two, **The Promise**. Click here to grab your copy!

Get a free book! To instantly receive *The Inn at Dolphin Bay*, the first novel in my most popular series, join my Reader Club at www.miakent.com/dolphin.

Thank you so much for your support!

Love,

Mia

ABOUT THE AUTHOR

Mia Kent is the author of clean, contemporary women's fiction and small-town romance. She writes heartfelt stories about love, friendship, happily ever after, and the importance of staying true to yourself.

She's been married for over a decade to her high school sweetheart, and when she isn't working on her next book, she's chasing around a toddler, crawling after an infant, and hiding from an eighty-pound tornado of dog love. Frankly, it's a wonder she writes at all.

To learn more about Mia's books, to join her Reader Club, or to send her a message, visit her website at www.miakent.com.

Printed in Great Britain
by Amazon